Dollar a Day

Gabriel Winston Lee, who goes by the name of Real, is a scion of an old Virginia family and fought as a cadet in the Civil War. Today, he's a gun for hire. Tom Easter enlists Real Lee for gun work protecting some Green Valley settlers, at the cowboy wages of a dollar a day.

Real is reticent but accepts when he hears Wolf Wilder and Finn McBride are also involved. Joined by Brewster and Jaime Sparrow the six men ride for the new town of Respite. Trouble, however, lies in wait as Ben Seffleck, a nemesis from Real's past, and Lillian Whitehead, his former lover, stand between Lee, his companions and peace in Green Valley. Will a dollar a day do the job?

Dollar a Day

Chuck Tyrell

A Black Horse Western

ROBERT HALE · LONDON

© Chuck Tyrell 2011
First published in Great Britain 2012

ISBN 978-0-7090-9310-7

Robert Hale Limited
Clerkenwell House
Clerkenwell Green
London EC1R 0HT

www.halebooks.com

Typeset by
Derek Doyle & Associates, Shaw Heath
Printed and bound in Great Britain by
CPI Antony Rowe, Chippenham and Eastbourne

1

'What brings you to Sunset, Tom?' Real Lee punctuated his question with a sip of Old Potrero, the best whiskey the Rose of Sharon had to offer.

'Got some gun work, Real. Interested?'

'Could be.' Real turned to face Tom Easter. The gunman wore his customary black – a black duster, black flat-rimmed hat, black vest, black trousers, black gun rig with silver conchos, and a nickel-plated Peacemaker with ebony grips. Real didn't have to go outside to know Tom Easter's coal black stallion was standing at the hitch rail. 'What's in it for me?' Real asked.

'Dollar a day and found.'

'Shee-it. That's not gun work, that's charity.'

'How much you making right now?'

Real grinned. 'You got me there. Only what I pick up at penny ante poker.'

A youngster burst through the batwings of the Rose of Sharon saloon. 'I'm looking for Real Lee,' he shouted. 'I hear he's the gunman in this burg. I can best him, I swear.'

'Go home, son,' Real said. 'This ain't a good day to die. No day is.'

The youngster dropped to a crouch, his hand hanging

like a claw over the handle of a Remington Army .45. 'Who're you to talk about dying?' His question sounded like a demand.

Real held his hands open at shoulder height, palms out, turned his back on the young gunman, walked to the end of the ornate bar and picked up the sawed-off Ithaca ten-gauge Shorty always had hanging there. Cocking the double hammers, he turned to face the youngster. 'I'm Real Lee, boy. I got nothing to prove, so if you don't want a belly full of double-aught buckshot, you'd better just settle down. How 'bout a drink?'

'Y-y-you're Real Lee?'

'That I am.'

'You ain't even wearing a gun.'

'Only wear one when I'm working.' Real gave the boy a genuine smile. 'Me and my friend Tom Easter were just going to sit down for a serious drink. Be honored if you'd care to join us.'

The youngster's jaw dropped. 'Tom Easter? The Texas gunman?'

'He prefers to be called the Texas barrister,' Real said. 'Will you join us? I'd rather have you as a friend than have you gunning for me.'

'You mean it?'

'I do.'

A smile lit up the youngster's face. 'Me. Friend to Real Lee and Tom Easter. Gol. Yeah. Pleasure.'

'Right over there, son.' Real pointed to a table in the center of the saloon. He took the bottle of Old Potrero in one hand and three glasses in the other. *Nothing like sharing a drink to weld a friendship*, Real thought. He beckoned to Tom Easter and the youngster to sit down, and poured the whiskey.

Tom picked his up, but the young man left the glass on the table.

'Got a problem drinking with me, boy?' Real put an edge on his voice.

'Oh no, Mr Lee. I'm honored. But . . .'

Real raised an eyebrow. Tom Easter downed his drink and set the glass down with a loud clonk. He gave the impression of a coiled spring even though he sat relaxed at the table.

The youngster sat looking at the glass of whiskey.

'What's your problem, son?' Real took a sip of his drink.

'Ummm. Well. I mean to say . . .'

'Spit it out, youngster.'

The young man raised a tortured face. 'My old man loved snake water. Whenever he came into a bit of money, he'd get pie-eyed. Then he'd beat my mom, and me, when I was younger. That drunk finally beat my mother to death. I killed him. I swore I'd never touch liquor as long as I live. It ain't that I got anything against you, Mr Lee, or you, Mr Easter, it's just that my pa was a drunkard so there's a chance I'd be one, too, if ever I started to drink . . . so, thank you, Real Lee, but no thanks.' The youngster let out the breath he'd been holding.

Real nodded. 'Makes sense.' He pushed his own half-empty glass away. 'Hey, Shorty,' he hollered. 'What've you got to drink that ain't booze?'

'Sarsaparilla,' Shorty shouted back.

'Bring some.'

'Be right there.' Shorty ducked behind the bar.

'Now. What's your name, son? And where are you from?' Real hitched his chair closer and leaned his elbows on the table.

'Lightning.'

7

Real just looked at the youngster for a long moment. 'Lightning?'

'Yep.'

'Lightning?' Real couldn't keep the incredulity from his voice.

The young man pushed his chair back and stood. 'You got a problem with my name? Well, let me tell you. That night, lightning struck the old cottonwood by the wagon I was born in, and my mother named me Lightning of God, 'cause none of us got hurt. I can't change that. I won't. Lightning I am. Lightning I'll always be.'

Shorty brought a big glass of frothy sarsaparilla to the table.

Real nodded slowly. 'Right. Lightning you are. Sit and drink up.'

Lightning settled back into his chair.

'What's your other name?'

'Only got one.'

'Your family name.'

'Oh. Brewster.'

'Lightning Brewster.' Real lifted his Stetson and ran a hand through strawberry hair flecked with early gray.

'What about the job?' Tom Easter asked.

'Depends on what for,' Real said.

'Range rovers getting set to drive settlers out of Green Valley.' Easter leaned forward, his eyes on Real's face.

'How many settlers?'

'Thirteen families. I figure somewhat more than fifty people, kids included.'

'Sell them guns and let them care for themselves.'

Easter shook his head. 'Religion says no.'

'Shee-it.'

'Uh-huh. Can't fight, but someone else can do the

8

fighting for them.'

'Shee-it,' Real said again.

'I don't cotton to people getting strong-armed off their legal land,' Easter said.

'Man oughta defend what's his,' Real said.

'Yeah, but some can't. Takes all kinds. What do you say? At least come with me to talk to them.'

'Green Valley?' The question came from Lightning Brewster.

Easter and Real looked at him. 'Yeah, Green Valley,' Easter said.

'I've been to Green Valley,' Lightning said, 'and I can shoot.'

'No fight for boys,' Easter said. 'Cyril Brocklin's the big rancher in those parts, and I hear he's hired Amos Dwyer up from Pecos country. Him and Tag Eidelbaur.'

Lightning said nothing, but his eyes took on an eager shine, and his lips parted as if in anticipation.

'Two of us ain't enough,' Real said. 'Who else you got in mind?'

'Falan Wilder, I reckon.'

'The Wolf's worth a dozen men, but he's got that outfit in Lone Pine Canyon now, and a newborn daughter. Think he's come?'

Easter shrugged. '*Quien sabe?*'

'Anyone else?'

'Phineas McBride.'

Real nodded. 'Shoulda known.'

'I know Green Valley, and I can shoot,' Lightning said. 'Can I go along?'

Neither Real nor Easter answered.

'When you leaving?'

'You in?'

'Got nothing better to do at the moment. When we leaving?'

'Soon as you're ready.'

'Dollar a day and found?'

Easter nodded. 'That's it,' he said.

'Who's paying for bullets?'

Easter shrugged. 'Bring your own.' He shoved his chair back. 'Let's give it a couple of hours,' he said. 'You get ready, then we'll ride. I'll be back.' He stood and strode from the Rose of Sharon. Every eye in the saloon marked his exit.

Real went to the polished bar and put the bottle of Old Potrero on the glistening surface. 'Keep that for me, Shorty, and give me my hoglegs.'

Shorty put the bottle in the hutch and pulled a gun rig from under the bar. He handed the rig to Real, who buckled it around his hips. At his right hand, a Colt Frontier rode high in a cutaway holster. On the left side, positioned for a right-hand cross draw, an 1878 Colt Police model, also .44 caliber.

Lightning Brewster followed Real through the batwings of the Rose of Sharon.

'Real Lee!' Three men stood in a line across the dusty street.

Real paused at the edge of the boardwalk. 'That you, Red?'

'It is.'

'Not man enough to come alone, then?'

'We want you dead, Real Lee. Man or woman or day-old babe, it don't make no difference. This is your last day.' The man in the middle did the talking, big and sun-burned, with oily black hair straggling from under his round-crowned hat.

'I got the man on the left,' Lightning said as he sidled off away from Real.

Real gave a slight nod. 'Red Skousen. If anyone dies today, you're sure to be one of them. Doesn't have to be this way, you know. Your brother came looking to make a name by besting Real Lee, but he died. No need for you to follow him.' Real stepped off the boardwalk and started walking swiftly toward the three men, his hands swinging naturally at his sides. Lightning followed a step and a half behind.

Skousen took a step back. 'Now Bert!' he hollered, and clawed for the pistol at his side.

Real ran three light steps to the right and dropped to one knee. A rifle cracked from a rooftop. Dust spurted on a line with where Real had been. Lightning proved his name. His Remington was out and yammering before anyone else could draw. The shooter on the roof toppled, then the man on the left, whose gun was yet only halfway out of its holster when Lightning's bullet took him in the throat.

Real's Frontier was out. 'Two dead, Red. Do you want more?'

'Gol damn right,' Red Skousen bawled. He raised his Colt for a shot, but a .44 caliber bullet from Real Lee's gun smashed into the center of his chest before he could pull the trigger.

Lightning killed the third man in the street.

'Damn, I hate this kind of thing,' Real said. 'Skousen didn't have to die.' He methodically ejected two spent shells from his Colt and inserted new cartridges from his belt.

Lightning reloaded his Remington and stuffed it back into the holster. 'Law's coming,' he said.

11

'Yeah,' Real said. 'Usually does.'

'Four dead men, Lee,' said the man with the badge on his vest.

'Coulda been me that's dead, Rencher.'

'Heard Red Skousen was gunning for you.'

'He found me. His mistake.'

'Real Lee. Four men dead here by your hand. That makes nigh on to a dozen since you come into town. A bit much, by any man's count.' Sheriff Rencher shifted the sawed-off shotgun so his right hand gripped the stock. 'Sunset was a peaceful town until you came,' he said. 'How long you planning to stay?'

Real grinned. 'Rencher, I purely cannot help it if men come looking to shoot it out with me. It's not like I was putting up posters, you know.'

Rencher frowned. 'How long, Lee?'

'I'm not welcome, then?'

'I'll rest easier without you here. Let's say that.'

'You're in luck, then. I'll be leaving later today.'

The sheriff actually showed a hint of a smile. 'Best news I've heard all day,' he said. 'Red and Billy Skousen are down, but you'd better keep an eye on your back trail. Sooner or later, Peggoty Skousen will come down that trail, and he's pure hell at gun work. Better than both his brothers put together.'

After the law, the next person to arrive was the undertaker. He cleared his throat. 'Umm, sheriff? Is the county paying for care of the deceased?'

Rencher threw an angry glance at Real Lee. 'Hmph. Yeah. County pays.'

'Come on, Lightning. We've got war to get ready for,' Real said.

2

Real Lee and Lightning Brewster waited for Tom Easter in front of the Rose of Sharon. Real had coffee in his saddle-bags along with four boxes of Colt .44-40 cartridges. His four-cup coffeepot dangled from the saddle strings. His sorrel whickered like he was anxious to get on the road.

'Just hang on, Sorry,' Real said. 'Tom'll be along any minute now.'

Lightning laughed. 'Do you talk to your horse all the time?'

Real turned, a serious look on his face. 'Don't make fun. You'll hurt his feelings. That horse listens to me better than most people do.'

'No guff?' Lightning widened his eyes in fake surprise. 'My Patches may be the dumbest critter on four legs, but she'll keep on going after everybody else is down and out. Toughest cayuse I ever seen.'

'Don't look big enough to carry a full-size man,' Real said, eyeing the little three-color paint.

'She's big enough to carry me all night and all day.' A touch of belligerence creeping into Lightning's voice.

Real lifted his hands, palms out. 'No offense meant. I reckon a horse is only as good as the man in the saddle anyway. And from what I've seen, you're better'n most.'

Tom Easter rode up on his big black. 'You ready, Real?'

'Me and the boy's ready to ride,' Real said.

'No fight for a boy,' Easter said.

'I'd like him to come along, Tom. That good enough?'

'Who's gonna change his diaper?'

Lightning faced Tom Easter full on. 'You want to have a try at this baby, Tom Easter? See how a big man like you stands against a little boy like me?'

Tom Easter put a hand to his Colt and found himself looking at the muzzle of Lightning Brewster's Remington.

'Don't do it, boy,' Real said. 'You'll be glad Tom Easter's along before this piece of work is over. Save your bullets. You'll likely need them.'

'He figures I'm some kind of little boy,' Lightning said. The Remington at the end of his outstretched arm pointed straight at Tom Easter's chest. No fancy shooting for this kid, Real thought.

'I said he could come, Tom. He helped me out earlier. Four men came shooting for me, one of them on the roof of Jenkins' store.'

'Four to one? That's about even odds against you, Real.'

'Lightning took out three of them.'

Easter looked at the youngster for a long moment, then gave a little nod. 'Dollar a day and found,' he said.

Lightning put his Remington away. 'Could I hit you for a couple of dollars advance pay?' he asked Easter.

'Advance pay?'

Lightning hung his head. 'Ain't got no money, Mr Easter. And I need to buy some bullets. Only got one left.'

Easter smiled. He dug a gold eagle from his pocket and flipped it to Lightning. 'Buy your ammunition, boy, and get a good meal. You can catch up with us on the Black

Canyon road.'

'Yes, sir, Mr Easter, I'll surely do that.'

'Let's ride, Real. The kid can come along after.'

Real Lee gathered the reins of his sorrel and climbed aboard. A Winchester '73 filled the right-hand saddle scabbard and a long-barrelled Ithaca ten-gauge stock stuck out from under his left-hand stirrup leather. In the off-side saddle-bag, along with the cartridges for his Colt and the Winchester, Real had stuffed fifty shotgun shells filled with double-aught buckshot. 'Got my coffee,' he said. 'I'm ready.'

Real Lee and Tom Easter met Finn McBride at Mormon Farm in Pleasant Valley. Wolf Wilder rode in later that night. By then, young Lightning Brewster hadn't caught up.

Easter had bought a slab of bacon and some biscuits from a Mormon housewife, and Real brewed coffee. Easter repeated the terms for Wilder. 'Dollar a day and found,' he said. 'Not all that much for gun-work.'

'Tom, you know I'd come to help you even if I had to pay my own way. I owe you that much for that time at Fort Whipple.'

Easter waved a hand. 'Just happened to be hanging around,' he said.

'Good thing for me,' said Wilder.

'Coffee's ready,' Real said. 'Grab a cupful and I'll brew up some more.'

Night fell in Pleasant Valley, which had earned its name by the tall Ponderosa pines, knee-high grass and sweet water from Hog Creek. Four hard men hunkered down around a hatful of fire. They were silent, each comfortable in the company of the others.

'I'll take first watch,' Wolf Wilder said. 'Like to do some

15

walking around anyway. Who'll take second turn?'

'That'd be me, I reckon,' Real Lee said. 'Midnight hours agree with me.'

'Wake me about four,' Easter said. 'Finn, you get a good night's sleep. You can make breakfast at first light.'

'Eli Jackson!' Three pistol shots punctuated the shout. 'Eli Jackson!'

The cabin door opened. A long spare man in a knee-length nightgown came out. 'What can I do for you gentlemen?' he asked.

'You've been warned off Cibie land, Jackson, and you're still here. Time has come to stop talking and start doing. I'm giving you five minutes. Get everything you want to save out of that shack. When your time's up, it's gonna burn.'

'But. But. I own this land. I have claim to it.'

'Cibie's run cattle here since before Jeffords made peace with Cochise. Mr Brockman ain't about to let no gaggle of pumpkin rollers cut off Little Green Valley Creek water. Out!'

'But—'

'Franks. Pour that coal oil.'

One of the riders dismounted with a gallon jug in his hand. He walked around the cabin, sloshing coal oil on its sides and splashing it on the planks of the little porch at the front door.

'Mr Duggan. You can't just burn a man's home,' Jackson cried.

'Watch me. You got three minutes.'

The lanky man disappeared into the cabin, shouting at his wife and children to wake up and get out.

Ace Duggan called another man. 'Winky. Go turn the

16

cow and calf out of the corral and lean-to. We're here to burn them out, not to kill good stock.'

'You got it, Ace.'

'Two minutes,' Duggan yelled. He struck a Lucifer and held it to a coal oil-soaked rag on the end of a stick. The fuel lit with a little whump.

'Light up, men,' he hollered.

In seconds, a dozen torches blazed. Horses sidled around, nervous at the flames.

'One minute!' Duggan held the torch aloft.

Jackson, a broomstick wife, and three children scuttled from the shack, arms laden with whatever they could lay their hands on in the seconds Bancroft had given them.

'Burn it!' Duggan tossed his torch. It arched through the cabin's single oiled paper window, and flames began eating at the cabin's insides.

The riders threw their torches at the oil-soaked siding and the porch. The fire rushed skyward, and one of Jackson's girls began to bawl.

'Take 'em away, Jackson,' Duggan shouted. 'There's nothing left for them here.

Behind the cabin, the lean-to stable also burned, though the pole corral stood intact. Duggan called his crew. 'Cibie riders to me. Let's move out.'

The riders thundered off, but Ace Duggan reined in his horse in front of Jackson and his family. 'Lesson to you and your flock,' he said. 'You all don't learn the lesson, we'll keep burning until the last of your homesteads is ashes.' He spurred the horse into a run to catch up with the others.

Lightning Brewster rode into camp just in time for breakfast. He now sported a Winchester in a saddle scabbard and a new Stetson.

'That eagle went a long way, boy,' Real Lee said.

Lightning grinned. 'Stakes,' he said. 'Played me a little poker. Couldn't go to war with no more than this old Remington Army.'

'Biscuits and bacon,' Finn McBride said. 'Coffee's just about ready.'

'Grew up on sow belly,' Lightning said. 'Show me to it.'

Finn handed him a biscuit and bacon sandwich, then a tin cup of coffee.

Lightning took big bite. 'Gumph,' he said.

'Not proper manners to speak with one's mouth full, son,' Finn said. 'Did your mother not teach you about manners?'

Lightning's face went sober. He chewed the mouthful of food and swallowed it. 'She taught me all she could, mister, but cholery took her before I turned six. Don't remember all that much about her. Just that she was soft, and she was always there.'

'Sorry,' Finn mumbled.

'Gather 'round,' Tom Easter said. 'I'll tell you all I know about what's going on.'

Five men stood close around the fire, sipping strong coffee from battered tin cups. Easter took a healthy gulp. 'Cyril Brockman came to Green Valley some time in the late '50s. He was a teamster with Amiel Whipple's survey expedition in '53 and probably got a chance to see the valley then.'

'That'll be the Cibie, then,' Wolf Wilder said. 'We ate a lot of Cibie beef at Camp Verde.'

'He sold beef and horses to Camp Verde and Camp Apache and even to Fort Whipple. His brand is CB Connected, but everyone calls his place the Cibie.'

18

'He runs the valley, then, I reckon,' Finn McBride said.

'Yeah, but he's getting old, too. He's worked his way through three wives. Only one daughter that I've heard of, and she's off to school or something.'

'Is that the problem?'

'Yes and no. Late spring a bunch of homesteaders took out claims on the upper end of Cherry Creek. Brockman didn't like it. Thing is, they're all of a bunch. Call themselves the Assembly of Christ. They follow a preacher by the name of Eli Jackson.'

'God botherers?' Real Lee said.

'You could say that. They all work together. Hold everything in common, though each family works its own land. They've been run out of Kansas and out of Arkansas. I reckon they're hunting a little peace,' Easter said.

'And they picked the Cibie range?'

Easter nodded.

'Excuse me, Mr Easter,' Lightning said. 'I can't help but wonder who of them Christians has got money to pay us a dollar a day and found.'

'You're not as dumb as you look, boy,' Easter said. His smile took the sting from his words. 'They're not paying.'

'Huh?'

'Hugh Freelock is one of the Assembly of Christ. In Arkansas, he married Angela Whiting. She converted to their church, but her pa still owns the biggest spread in north Texas. He's paying us to watch out for his daughter, and that means watching out for the whole bunch – all or nothing.'

'Shee-it,' Real said.

'Anyone that wants, can leave right now,' Easter said.

'What's your plan?' Wilder threw the dregs of his coffee into the fire, which hissed in response.

'I reckon we should talk to Cyril Brockman first off,' Easter said.

Five men rode out of Pleasant Valley, picking a trail that lay north of Potato Butte. Easter let Wilder take the lead. This was his country and he'd scouted for the Army at least a dozen years.

Wilder sat his pale brindle grulla with the slouch of a rider born and bred on the Great Plains. Real Lee gigged his sorrel up alongside Wilder. 'What do you figure, Wolf? You heard anything about this spat?'

Wilder kept his eyes moving across the country, checking shadowed copses, watching the skyline, and looking for likely hideyholes. 'Dunno, Real,' he said, 'but I do know Cyril Brockman. He's a good neighbor. A tough man, no-nonsense. Moves quick. But I've always found him fair. Ask me, and I'll say there's something more than just some homesteaders staking out a piece of his range.'

Real and Wilder rode on in silence. A redtail hawk screeched from his lookout high atop a tall Ponderosa. 'There'll be a nest in that tree,' Wilder said. 'Hawks and men – all the same: protect the nest first.'

'Wonder if those homesteaders will spark a fight?'

'Count on it. But who's in the right?'

'Yeah. Who?'

Wilder pointed to a cut in the rambling wall of hills to the north. 'That's where Walnut Creek goes through. It'll get us over on to Tonto Creek, then it's just a hoop and a holler to Little Green Valley Creek. Brockman's Cibie headquarters are on high ground at the fork of Tonto and Little Green Valley Creek.'

Wilder and Lee pulled up to wait for the others.

'Three, four hours to the Cibie if we move right along,' Wilder said. 'That'll put us there around sunset.' He looked at Easter. 'You want to go in at dark? Or would morning be a better idea?'

'Is there a good place to camp close by?' Easter asked.

Wilder pointed at the cut. 'Once we get through that, there's some good grass along Tonto Creek. Give the horses time to graze if we stay the night.'

'Lead on,' Easter said. 'Your judgment's good enough for me.'

They rode in a line through the cut made by Walnut Creek – Wilder on his pale grulla, Real Lee and his red sorrel, Tom Easter with black clothing and horse, Finn McBride riding a white appaloosa with bulging oversized saddle-bags, and Lightning Brewster astraddle his three-color paint – red, white, and black.

Wilder picked a sheltered cienega a hundred yards or so back from Tonto Creek. They ate the last of the biscuits and bacon and had two cups of coffee each. Not long after dark, an owl hooted. 'Be back directly,' Wilder said. He took two steps into the scrub and disappeared.

'What's that all about?' Lightning said to Real.

'The Wolf don't miss a thing,' Real said. 'I reckon he wants to talk with that owl.'

'Owl?'

'Yeah. Didn't you hear it?'

'I hear owls all the time. Country's full of them.'

'Not that kind.'

'What kind?'

'Two-legged kind.'

'How'd you know that?'

Real grinned. 'I know Wolf Wilder,' he said.

Lightning stared off in the direction Wilder disappeared. 'Two-legged owl,' he muttered. 'Every owl I ever saw only had two legs.'

21

Wilder didn't come back alone. He pushed through the scrub with a dark young man in a poncho made from a wool Navajo rug. The youngster hung back as Wilder walked over to Tom Easter.

'What's up, Wolf?'

'My ranch hand Jaime Sparrow's been watching Green Valley,' Wilder said.

'And?'

'A cabin's burning.'

3

Cyril Brockman was once a large man. Now his withered legs weighed next to nothing and his lack of appetite had reduced his former bulk to little more than translucent skin stretched over his skeleton.

Brockman's body no longer did his bidding, but his brain still worked, most of the time. He knew Ace Duggan could take care of the Cibie, and he knew something was happening, he just didn't know what. Ace always did what Brockman asked, or it seemed that way. Since he'd lost the use of his legs when a horse fell on him, he'd not been able to ride to inspect his range. He trusted Ace to run the ranch like he trusted Ah Bim to get him around the house and get him the opium he needed to keep the pain at bay. These days, the pain in his gut was worse than the pain in his back.

'Ah Bim,' he hollered.

'Yes, massa.'

'A pipe, Ah Bim. Goddamn gut hurts like hell.'

'Yes, massa. Ah Bim think maybe massa should eat some food before the pipe, eh?'

'Get the goddamn pipe, you Chinaman asshole.'

'Yes, massa.'

'Don't let anyone in until I'm feeling better.' He wondered what Sybil would think when she came home from school in St Louis.

A dark room at the back of the house held a single bunk with a low table at its head. Ah Bim laid out the pipe with its dark brown pea of opium and lit the candle Brockman used to heat the bowl and vaporize the little bead of poppy residue.

Once Brockman had felt better in fifteen minutes or so, and it didn't even take a whole pea. Now it took two peas and just short of an hour to set things right.

Brockman had a chair with wheels on it for getting around the house, but he couldn't ride a horse without being tied in the saddle. He was worthless to the Cibie and had no idea what was happening at the ranch. He goddamn hurt. All the time, he hurt. Except for a couple of hours after smoking Ah Bim's little brown peas. He never let anyone in the house until after he'd smoked the peas. Never.

The thirteen Elders of the Assembly of Christ gathered at the smoking remains of Eli Jackson's cabin.

'The gospel of Christ is one of love,' he said. 'No one should harbor thoughts of revenge for this. It is just one more trial of faith that our Lord has seen fit to place upon us.'

'But Pastor—'

'No thoughts of revenge,' Jackson intoned. 'Instead, think of the dam. If we are to survive, we must have irrigation water. Although we can haul enough from the creek for truck gardens, we must have water for wheat and corn and rye and alfalfa. Don't worry about one cabin gone up in flames. Worry about completing the dam.'

'As you say, Pastor.'

'Gather round, brothers and sisters. Let us pray.'

Thirteen families knelt in a circle around the pastor, who removed his black hat and gazed at the heavens. 'Our Father which art in Heaven, hallowed by Thy name,' he said, calling on Christ's example of prayer. 'Thy kingdom come, Thy will be done, on earth as it is in heaven. Give us this day our daily bread and forgive us our trespasses as we forgive those who trespass against us.' Jackson paused. 'And what we need especially, Lord, is help in getting our irrigation dam in place. If Thee could just keep Satan's forces at bay while we work, this corner of Thy vineyard would bloom as a rose. . . .

'For Thine is the kingdom, and the power, and the glory, forever and ever. In Christ's name. Amen.'

'Amen,' echoed the Assembly.

'Remember,' Jackson said, 'when you pray, pray like everything is up to the Lord; when you work, work like everything is up to you. Now, let's get that dam built so God can bless our crops with water.'

'Amen,' the Assembly said.

The Assembly of Christ picked a place where Little Green Valley Creek ran between two sandstone banks that pinched like a thumb and forefinger. North of the pinchers, a small meadow opened up before the stream ran into the mountains around Diamond Point. Damming the pincher point would back water up into the meadow and make a lake of several hundred acres. From that lake, the community could draw all the water they needed for farming, and the overflow would keep Little Green Valley Creek running, or so they thought.

'Brethren, back to the dam. Sisters, tend to your gardens and care for your homes.'

Men began to leave the circle to ready the teams.

'Brother Lambert,' Jackson called.

A tall broad-shouldered man in homespun linsey-woolsey shirt, floppy hat, bib overalls, and old leather boots stopped without turning around.

'Brother Lambert?'

'I hear you, preacher. And my name's Walt. I'm no brother of yours.' Still, Walt Lambert didn't move.

'Brother Walt,' Jackson said, 'I'd be obliged if you'd take charge of building the dam. I can listen to the Lord, but rocks confound me. We need to get the dam built while there's still time to plant.'

Lambert's shoulders hunched as if he were expecting Jackson to hit him.

'Sister Maggie will be proud of you,' Jackson said, knowing that Walt Lambert was with the Community only because he loved his wife and she believed.

'I hear you, preacher,' Lambert said again. 'But will your band of brothers listen when I try to tell them what to do?'

'They will. They obey the word of the Lord.'

Lambert shrugged. 'If they listen and work like Hell, we can get your dam built,' he said.

'If you please, Brother Walt.'

Jackson walked to the head of the wagons the men had lined out, ready to go. Raising his voice, he called out. 'Brethren, listen to the word of the Lord. Brother Walt Lambert, a non-believer, shall lead the dam builders. Brother Walt studied the craft at the United States Military Academy and sharpened his skills as an officer in the Army Corps of Engineers. He left the government's employ and joined our Assembly because of Sister Margaret, his loving wife. The Lord works in mysterious ways. Brother Walt can

26

get the Lord's dam built. I know without a doubt that each of you brethren will do your utmost to help. God be with you. Amen.'

'Amen,' the men automatically chorused.

Real Lee rode Sorry a good fifty yards behind Wolf Wilder and the slim young man he called Sparrow. What had started out as four-man gun work had now turned into a six-man operation. He chewed on his cheek as he mulled the situation. He flicked a glance at Lightning, who rode head down, hat low over his eyes. He could be sleeping, but Real doubted it. Tom Easter and Finn McBride brought up the rear.

Easter had first said they'd go to see Cyril Brockman, but news of the burning cabin changed his mind. Real didn't care one way or the other. Gun work was gun work, and it didn't make much difference where it started.

Up ahead, a lone muley doe broke cover and bounded away. Wolf Wilder snaked his Winchester out and brought the doe down with a single shot from his seat on the brindle grulla.

'Lucky shot,' Lightning said.

'Lucky, my ass. Wolf don't make lucky shots. That Winchester's a one-in-a-thousand, but this Cheyenne half-breed makes it shoot like it was one in a million. Wolf hits what he shoots at. If he can't, he don't shoot.'

A calculating look crept into Lightning's eyes. 'How's he with a six-shooter? Can he beat you? Or Tom Easter?'

'Never tried him. Never want to. He use'nt to carry a six-gun, but after some trouble over at Lone Pine Canyon, he took to toting a Rogers & Spencer. He don't get it out very fast, but when he pulls the trigger, the bullet damn well goes where he wants it to.'

Lightning nodded, but didn't say anything more. He still looked like he wanted to try Wolf Wilder's hand.

The men gathered around the dead mule deer. 'If we're going calling, best we take something along,' Wilder said. Sparrow slipped off his gray mare and went to work on the deer with a big Bowie knife. He slit the doe's throat and began rolling her, bleeding her out so the meat would last longer. Then he cut away the hindquarters, slicing through the hip joint and leaving the backbone intact. He slit the hocks and threaded a piggin string through each. One quarter he handed to Wilder, the other he hung from his saddle horn. He left the rest of the doe for the varmints.

Wilder led the party over a hogback and down into Green Valley. The land spread out for miles. Willows and alders marked the course of Little Green Valley Creek, and cattle browsed on the tall grass. Wilder pulled up to wait for the others.

'Looks like Brockman got himself a big Hereford bull,' Wilder said. 'That'll put beef on the calves of them rangy Mexican cows he's been running.'

'Whereabouts are the settlers?' Tom Easter asked.

'Sparrow tells me they're way over on the northwest end of the valley, across the creek. The place can hardly be called Cibie range at all,' he said.

'Let's go,' Easter said.

Wilder nodded at Sparrow. 'He'll take the lead,' he said, and signed to Sparrow. The young man gigged his mare off up the eastern edge of the valley. The four horsemen followed, and Lightning drew up the rear.

Sparrow led them some twenty miles northwards before crossing Little Green Valley Creek and riding over a low rise that overlooked the settlers' claims.

The smoldering remains of a cabin lay in the center of the little community, and while each family's cabin stood on its claim, as required by law, it was built as close to the central one as possible.

'Let's go get the lay of the land,' said Easter as he urged his big black down the rise toward the community.

By the time the horsemen reached the remains of the cabin, half a dozen men and a gaggle of women and children had gathered to meet them.

Tom Easter rode out front, his hands on the saddlehorn. Wilder and Sparrow stayed back about ten feet and off to the left. Real Lee was at Easter's right stirrup with Lightning Brewster half a horse length behind. Finn McBride brought up the rear, a good way to the right.

A tall gangly man with chin whiskers and a gaunt, underfed look stepped out to meet the riders. 'I'll be Eli Jackson,' he said. 'I'm the pastor of the Assembly of Christ.'

'Who burned your cabin?' Easter asked.

'Do you horsemen come a-burning, too?' asked Jackson.

'Do we look like strongarms?'

'You look like death,' Jackson said. 'I've seen you through the eyes of Saint John the Revelator. You,' he pointed at Finn McBride, 'the first rider on a white horse. You,' his finger sought Real Lee, 'the second rider on a red horse. You,' the finger went to Easter, 'the third rider on a black horse, and you,' he said, pointing at Wolf Wilder, 'the fourth rider, death, on a pale horse. I know you, horsemen, and I fear you bring no good.'

Tom Easter spoke in a quiet voice that held a hard edge. 'Would Hugh Freelock be here?'

'Brother Hugh is with those who are building our irrigation dam.'

'How about Angela Freelock, then?'

A bonneted young woman spoke. 'I am Angela Freelock,' she said.

Tom Easter raised a finger to the brim of his black hat. 'Tom Easter is the name, ma'am. Arthur Whiting asked us to ride over to see that you stayed safe.'

'Pa?'

Easter nodded.

Tears welled in the woman's eyes. Her voice trembled as she spoke, but her words were brave. 'All is well here, Mr Easter. The Lord God watches over his flock.'

Easter gazed for a long moment at the smoldering remains of the cabin. 'Yes, I can see that,' he said. 'But if it's just the same with you, we'll stick around for a while. I promised Arthur we would.'

'The Assembly is one,' Jackson said. 'While we can't tell you where or when to make camp, we cannot invite you into our midst unless you have some interest in our teachings. I'm sure you understand.'

'Actually, I don't,' Easter said. 'In this country, a man is free to believe what he wants, long as he don't try to force it on anybody else.'

Jackson nodded. 'We only wish to be left alone, to live and worship according to God's will.'

'Who burned your cabin?'

'Roughnecks.'

'What for?'

'We were told to leave.'

'Will you?'

Jackson said nothing.

Easter nodded. 'Don't you worry, Miss Angela, We'll be around.'

'Mister?' A voice called out.

Easter turned his attention to a tall thin girl with hair as black as his stud horse.

'Mister?'

'Yes ma'am.'

'The man who burned our home is named Ace Duggan.'

'He just came and burned you out?'

'No. First he came and warned us to leave.'

'When?'

'When we were holding Sabbath services. Five days ago.'

Easter's eyes sharpened. 'How many men?'

'No need to tell all, Ruth,' Jackson said.

The girl turned on the preacher. 'Father, how many times have you told us that the Lord works in mysterious ways His wonders to perform? How many times? Who is to say that Mr Easter and his friends are not the hand of God in the day of our tribulation?'

Easter's black stallion stirred uneasily, sidestepping, but when Easter said, 'Hold up, Devil,' the horse settled down. 'Do you know who this Ace Duggan is?' he asked the girl.

'A destroyer,' she said. 'He said to get the Assembly of Christ off Cibie range, even though we have filed legal claims on this land at Globe City.'

'Cyril Brockman's been in this valley a long time,' Easter said. 'Probably figures it's his.' He backed Devil away. 'We'll be back,' he said. 'Wolf, might be a good idea if you left that meat with the preacher.'

Wolf Wilder sidled his horse up to the clot of people. 'Me and Sparrow's got haunches of mule deer for you,' he said.

'Stan. Josiah. Take the offerings,' Jackson said. 'Our

31

thanks to you, death rider. Perhaps your offering will save lives. God only knows.' The men accepted the haunches of venison.

Real Lee watched through slitted eyes. Something told him this job of gun work wasn't going to be a push over.

4

Tom Easter pitched their camp at the top of the hogback rise, east of the Assembly farms. 'Best we let them see we're here,' he said. The fire was larger than any of the horsemen would have used on the trail, built to be seen rather than to warm. Jaime Sparrow disappeared into the night. Lightning Brewster watched him go, then followed a few minutes later. He left his new hat and boots in camp after changing to moccasins from his saddle-bags.

'All right if that young gunhand goes after Sparrow?' Real asked Wolf Wilder.

The Wolf smiled. 'The boy'll not see Sparrow unless he allows it.'

'Don't sell the youngster short. He's hell on wheels, and he wasn't born yesterday either.'

'We'll see,' Wilder said.

Real changed the subject. 'How's things going at Lone Pine?'

'The mares from up on the Prieta threw their first foals this spring,' Wilder said. 'And me and Blessing, we had our first, too.'

Real raised his eyebrows. 'Hadn't heard you were in a family way.'

Wilder grinned. 'Hard to stay out of the family way with a woman like Blessing,' he said.

'And. . . .'

'And what?'

'Don't hold back.'

Wilder looked bewildered. 'What do you mean? I'm not holding nothing back.'

'Well?'

'Dammit Real. Of you've got a question, just out and ask it. No reason to keep beating around the bush.'

'Which was it?'

'Which was what?' Wilder's voice started to take on an edge.

'Well, was the kid a wrangler or a biscuit maker?'

'Oh.' Wilder's eyes hinted at mirth but his face was dead still. 'Me and Blessing have a daughter,' he said. 'Her name is Gracious.'

Real smiled. He wondered what it would be like to want to stick with one woman and maybe have kids with her.

Sparrow and Lightning showed at the fire when it was down to coals and the horsemen were sipping their last cups of coffee.

Sparrow looked at Lightning and gave a little nod.

'People watching the Assembly,' Lightning said.

Tom Easter stood up. 'How many?'

'We seen three. May be more.'

'Wolf, do me a favor?'

'Sure.'

'Bring me one of those watchers.'

Wilder nodded. He too donned moccasins and fitted a strange-looking knife to the small of his back. He signed to Sparrow, and Sparrow beckoned to Lightning. The youngster shed his gun rig and shoved the Remington Army into

34

his waistband. He looked at Sparrow. 'Ready,' he said. The three men faded into the night.

'That youngster never fails to surprise me,' Real said.

Lambert knew the moment he saw the site that construction of a proper dam would take more than a year to build, maybe two. But it wouldn't get built if they didn't start. All he had to work with was eight men, including himself, 12-pound sledges, rock chisels, a couple of drills, crowbars, fifty feet of chain, determination, and a few odds and ends. It would have to do.

He pointed at a red sandstone cliff rising in the west. 'We'll tear down that mountain to build our dam,' he said. 'Let's go take a look.'

The cliff had three sandstone spires rising before it. Lambert walked around each spire, eyeballing it. The spires, along with loose boulders nearby, would provide a decent foundation for the crescent-shaped gravity dam he saw in his mind.

'Be good if we had enough powder to blow these down,' he said, half to himself. Then, 'We'll just have to treat these spires like big trees. Get the crowbars and shovels.'

The men took turns hacking the support from under the southernmost spire. It stood forty feet high and ten feet through at the bottom, and a man could chip away at the sandstone with a crowbar or a 5-pound sledge and chisel, but progress came almighty slow.

Lambert took his turn with the men, smashing at the notch with sledge and chisel. And when it came time to set up camp, he pitched in, doing more than his share. Still, only a couple of the men spoke to him, and Deacon James led the hymn singing and prayer circle. Lambert didn't join them. He sat alone, careful not to stare at the fire, and thought about the dam he'd promised to build.

He'd heard of the dam the Mormons put across the Little Colorado about ten miles downstream from Horsehead Crossing. They'd laid down brush and sunk it into the sand of the river bottom by piling rocks and dirt on top of it. Took them just over two months to build the dam and a year for it to wash away.

The Assembly's dam was a horse of a different color because the stream bottom was on rock at the dam site, the breadth between the banks was less than fifty yards, and Little Green Valley Creek wasn't fed by the Puerco and Zuni rivers and two hundred miles of drainage that stretched into the White Mountains. The Assembly's dam would get no muddy flash floods like the ones that came down the Little Colorado almost every year. Lambert knew how the dam should be built, and he knew how to make it last.

'Brother Lambert?' Hugh Freelock's voice broke into Lambert's planning.

Lambert looked up.

'Mind if I sit with you for a while?' Freelock asked.

'Help yourself.'

The young man sat. For some moments, he said nothing. 'Brother Lambert?'

'My name's Walt.'

Freelock nodded. 'Brother Walt,' he said.

Lambert frowned at the 'brother' but let it ride.

Freelock heaved a sigh. 'Seems we didn't make much progress today, did we?'

'Well enough.'

'We need that water real soon,' he said. 'I reckon there's no way to hurry things up, though.' The young man's shoulders rounded like he was carrying the whole Assembly on his back.

'What's bothering you, Freelock?'

Tears showed in the young man's eyes, but he blinked them away before they fell. 'It's Angela, Brother Walt.'

'What's the problem? She's not like me. She converted.'

'We're going to have a baby.'

'Most married folks do.'

'But what have I got to offer?'

Lambert gave Freelock a sharp look. 'What did your parents give you, then?'

'That's it,' he said. 'Pastor Jackson heard the voice of God in a battle during the war. He started the Assembly of Christ as soon as it was over. My folks joined when I was only three, so this is all I've ever known.'

'Don't see your folks around.'

Freelock shook his head. 'Pa was killed in the Potter Creek massacre when the Kansas mob shot up the Assembly camp. We was leaving, and they still came shooting. Ma died that winter.'

' 'S too bad.' Lambert knew about losing family. His had stood in the way of J.E.B. Stuart as he rode to join the battle at Gettysburg. Civilians weren't supposed to die, but they did. Lambert's father fell with the cavalry at Middleburg, a full colonel. His mother died in her kitchen, hit by a chance bullet from Confederate guns. Their deaths paved Lambert's way into West Point.

Freelock sniffed. 'Pastor Jackson always said the Assembly was the only true path of God. Other pastors didn't like to hear that. Believers pay a price. A high one. But what's true is true.' He sighed. 'So I can offer my child Eli Jackson's truth, and not much else. Don't even know how we'll feed the little one.'

'You can only do the best you can.'

'Yeah. But it don't seem like enough.'

Lambert sat silent for some time, considering what he was going to say. Finally he took a breath. 'You could always take Angela back to Texas,' he said.

Sparrow and Lightning brought the first man back to the horsemen's fire. 'Hello the fire,' came a call from Lightning. 'Three men coming in. Two friendly.' The young men pushed a slight red-haired man into the circle of light shed by the fire.

Real Lee recognized the man at once. 'I killed your brother in Sunset the other day,' he said. 'What in hell are you doing sneaking around a bunch of god-botherers?' Real glanced at Tom Easter. 'Wouldn't expect Peg Skousen to be here, would you?'

'Who cares, long as we get a handle on what's going on.' Easter drew his Colt and reached for a hold on Skousen's shirt collar. Jerking the seedy roughneck close, he shoved the muzzle of his six-gun into the soft flesh under Skousen's jaw. The man's eyes bulged, whites showing all around.

'Who's paying the bills, owlhoot?' Easter's tone of voice said he'd as soon pull the trigger as mess around playing footsie with snide answers. 'Who!'

Skousen gurgled.

Easter pulled back on the Colt enough for Skousen to answer.

'Hell, I don't know,' he said. 'Tom Ranklin at Big Johney Gulch passed out cash to a bunch of us. Don't know who paid him.'

'Who you taking orders from?'

'Pearson Tate.'

'Pearson Tate? Last I heard, he was a marshal at Mobeetie.'

'He ain't no marshal now.' Skousen hacked to clear his throat.

'So what's a stumblefoot like you doing wandering around in the dark?'

'Tate seen your fire on the hill and wondered who made it. He sent me to see, and he wanted me to check on the Amen crowd, while I was out.'

'And you let two boys take you?' Easter snorted.

Skousen seemed to relax. Perhaps he decided Easter wasn't going to kill him. 'Them two ain't boys, they're ghosts. They snaked up on me clean as a whistle, and the dark kid's Bowie talks loud and clear. I weren't about to get chopped up. I come along, easy like.' Then he looked at Real Lee. 'Lee, we got a score to settle, me and you. Now's not the time, but the time will come, count on it.'

'I won't be hiding when you come, Peg.'

Tom Easter holstered his Colt. 'Let's see what the Wolf brings in,' he said. He shoved Skousen toward Lightning. 'Stake him out,' he said. 'Sparrow can show you how.'

'I know how,' Lightning said. 'Come on, Sparrow.'

Real Lee watched the young men cut, trim, and drive four stakes into the hard earth, then spread-eagle Peggoty Skousen on the ground and tie each of his limbs to a stake. 'All we need now is a red anthill,' Real mumbled to himself. Still, he understood Easter's thinking. A staked-out man is not likely to get away.

'Coming in.' Wilder spoke in a natural voice, but somehow it carried. He pushed a tall, broad-shouldered young man who wore cowboy gear – leather vest, stovepipe chaps, spurs that jingled with every step, and an old Colt in a handmade holster. Wilder hadn't even bothered to take the weapon.

'Was this man sneaking around?' Easter asked.

Wilder smiled. 'Nah. He come riding by, pretty as you please. I just kinda stepped out and stopped him.'

Easter turned on the cowboy. 'How come you to be riding around this neck of the woods in the middle of the night?'

The cowboy hung his head, eyes on the ground. 'It ain't nothing,' he said, his voice hardly more than a whisper.

'Cowboys don't go for joy rides at night,' Easter said. 'Come clean now. First off, tell us who you are and who you ride for.'

'Horse is branded CB,' Wilder said.

'I'm Roland Grieves. I been living at the Cibie since my folks died in '75. Mr Brockman's always took my side of things. I. . . .'

'How old are you, boy?'

'Fifteen . . . going on sixteen.'

'Only two reasons I know why a cowboy'd be out riding at midnight,' Real said. 'One's watching a bedded-down herd. The other's a woman. I'm betting Rolly here is riding to see a woman.'

Rolly hung his head.

'A woman, then. Eh, boy?' Easter's voice could have cut leather.

'She ain't like them women at the Nugget in Payson,' he said. 'She's God-fearing. A woman oughta be God-fearing.'

'The girl got a name?'

Rolly clamped his lips together and shook his head.

'What would Brockman say if he knew you was sniffing around the god-botherers' place?'

Rolly lifted his head, a sad look on his face. 'These days

40

Mr Brockman don't care about much,' he said in a sorrowful voice. 'He can't walk no more. I reckon he's kinda maybe lost hope or something.'

'Shee-it,' Real Lee said. 'Look, youngster. You're a long way from the Cibie. Anyone know you're here?'

Rolly nodded. 'Ace reckons I'm checking the line shack over by the rim,' he said. 'I did that, but I figured to see her before I rode back.'

'Her?' Real raised an eyebrow. Who is "her"?'

Rolly Grieves answered in a very small voice. 'Ruth Jackson.'

5

The horsemen watched over the Assembly almost the entire morning. Smoke rose from a central cooking fire just after dawn, and before the sun had gotten more than a finger's breadth above the horizon, Jackson's followers had scattered. Some went to the fields. Others did chores around their cabins. Three worked at cleaning up the remains of Jackson's burned-out cabin. There was no sign of cowboys or gunmen.

As they hunkered down around the coals left from the breakfast fire, Tom Easter outlined the day.

'Real, be obliged if you and Finn could ride upstream and have a look at the dam the Assembly's supposed to be building.'

'Can do,' Real said. 'You OK riding with me, Finn?'

McBride grinned. 'I may wear bib overalls, gunny, but my Spencer shoots same as your Colt and the bullets hit where I'm pointing. We'll get along.'

Real laughed. 'You won't find me calling out Finn McBride,' he said. 'As likely to get a lapful of dynamite as a slug in the belly.'

'Just as long as you understand,' McBride chuckled.

'Good to be riding with you again, Real, though things have changed since then.'

'They have.' Real glanced at Lightning. 'You coming?'

Lightning looked embarrassed. 'It's not that I wouldn't be honored to ride with you, Mr Lee. It's just that, well, me and Sparrow, we been talking, and we figure to do some snaking around. See if we can't find where the skunk is holed up. Things don't smell quite right around here. If that's OK with you, Mr Wilder.' Lightning took a big breath.

Easter glanced at Wilder, who gave a slight nod. 'Don't get yourselves in trouble,' he said.

'Umm. Could we take Rolly along?' Lightning asked. 'We'll get him back to the Cibie before long.'

Easter turned to Rolly. 'What do you think of that?' He asked.

'I oughta be shagging back to the Cibie, but—'

'He ain't seen his girl yet, Mr Easter. Rolly come all the way out here to see her, but he ain't. We'll make sure he does, before he goes back.'

Easter's face was stern, but there was a twinkle in his eyes. 'All right. But Rolly's you guys' responsibility, y'hear?'

'Yes, sir,' Lightning said.

'Me and Wolf Wilder'll ride to the Cibie direct,' Easter said. 'See if we can't pin down what's going on. From what Rolly says, and from what Peg Skousen told us, Brockman don't seem to be at the back of this trouble.'

Easter walked over to where Skousen lay spread-eagled on the ground, an old sock stuffed in his mouth. He looked down at the gunhand for a long moment, then dug in his pocket for a Barlow knife.

'You listen to me, Skousen. I'm cutting you loose. And I'll give you back your gun. I reckon your plug's tied off in the junipers somewhere, else you'll walk. Either way, you tell Preston Tate that Tom Easter said to lay off the Assembly, else he'll have to answer to me and those who ride with me. You got that?'

Skousen nodded vigorously, and Easter cut the thongs that held him to the stakes.

Lightning came over with Skousen's hat and gun. 'I ride with Mr Easter,' he said, 'and who stands against Real Lee stands against me.'

He tossed the hat and gun on the ground at Skousen's feet. 'Me and Sparrow snaked up on you without you ever knowing we was around. You never know, Skousen, when one of us will be there in the night. Sparrow's Bowie is more than unusual sharp, and my six-gun don't never miss.' He turned his back on Skousen and walked away.

Skousen grabbed the hat and crammed it on his head.

'Be careful how you pick up that iron,' Real Lee said.

Skousen hesitated. 'It ain't like I'm scared of you, Lee. It just ain't the right time.' He leaned down and grasped the gun rig with his hand around the cylinder of the walnut-handled .45. He looped the cartridge belt over his shoulder and walked westwards off the hogback without another word.

'The day will come,' Real Lee said. Then, 'Come on, Finn. Let's go have a look at the God-botherers' damn dam.'

Ace Duggan stood at the front door of the big Cibie ranch house. 'Here to report to Mr Brockman,' he said to the Chinaman, whose name he never could remember. It always reminded him of a sneeze. Ah Ah . . . something or other.

The Chinaman left him standing there, hat in hand, like some kind of worthless grunt. Who the Hell did that Chinaman think ran the Cibie anyway.? Where did he think this spread would be if not for Ace Duggan, huh?

'Come in, massa,' the Chinaman said.

Ace entered the dark front room. It smelled smoky and kind of sweet. Not like tobacco smoke either. Cyril Brockman sat in his wheeled chair with his elbows on the dining table. His eyes were dark holes sunk into his skull and his grin reminded Ace of an old skull he'd found once in a cliff dwelling down by Silver City in New Mexico.

'What is it, Ace?' Brockman's tone was syrupy. His smile seemed pasted on, and his eyes wandered back and forth, like maybe he couldn't focus right.

'Came to tell you what's going on, Boss, like always.'

'Always? Oh. Yes. Surely. Always. . . .' Brockman looked around. His eyes rested on the Chinaman, and he seemed reassured. 'Yes?' he said.

'Boss, we're losing cattle. I figured it were the Assembly at first, but now I'm not sure. And I reckon maybe we don't need all those gunhands who follow Pearson Tate.'

'Didn't you say the Christians were building a dam?'

'Yes.'

'I thought so. Dam, eh?'

'Don't reckon the dam'll hurt, Boss. May even help some, if water ever gets short.'

'Damn Christians,' Brockman said.

'They're legal, Boss. We run 'em out with firepower, and Sheriff Reynolds'll be on our necks.'

'Never liked to bother God about things,' Brockman said. 'Men are bother enough.'

45

'Yes, Boss. What shall I do about them?'

'Shits. Squatters. On my land. Building a dam without so much as a by-your-leave. Not neighborly.' Brockman stopped to draw deep rasping breaths into his lungs.

'Don't think we should be pushing them, Boss.'

'What did you say about Pearson? Who's that?'

'You told me to hire guns, Boss. Pearson Tate's segundo to Tom Ranklin up at Big Johney Gulch. He don't pay much attention to what I say, Boss. I don't like having those gunnies around.'

'Gotta run the god-botherers off. We do. My range. Been here since '56. Ace? You listening?'

'Yes, Boss.'

'I want them Christians gone.'

'Boss? It's ain't '56 no more. It's closer to '86. Green Valley's part of Gila County now, Boss. We'd best stay away from gun work.'

Brockman's chin rested on his scrawny chest.

Ace looked at the Chinaman. He shook his head, walked over to take hold of the posts on Brockman's wheeled chair and trundle him into a back room.

Two hours put Real Lee and Finn McBride at the dam site. There were signs which said men, horses, and wagons had been there, but the site was bare.

The water in Little Green Valley Creek ran clear, moving swiftly across the rocky bottom. Real reined Sorry to a pool at one side and let him drink his fill. He cocked a leg over the saddlehorn, dug in his vest pocket for the makings, and rolled himself a smoke. Not often that he used tobacco, but he figured it helped him think. He lit up with a lucifer and studied the country as he smoked.

The dam site seemed obvious to Real, if someone wanted to build a dam, that is. The dam, placed across the rocky narrows, would back up water into a small circular swale that looked almost like a caldera.

But where were the builders?

While Real smoked, Finn walked his white appaloosa around the site, splashing back and forth across the creek, making a slightly wider circle with each go-round. Finally he pulled up. 'Real,' he hollered, 'they took off up the canyon.'

Real snuffed out his smoke and rolled the remains in his fingers, scattering the tobacco and shredding the paper. He punched Sorry with his heels. The sorrel took the hint, stopped cropping grass, and walked carefully across the rocky shallows.

Finn pointed to wagon tracks headed northwest. 'We follow that trail and we'll find those dam builders,' he said.

'Let's do it.'

The dam builders didn't have any pickets set, so Real and Finn rode right up to the work site, hands crossed over their saddlehorns.

Real called out. 'Hello-o-o-o.'

The racket continued.

He raised his voice and called again.

A tall straight-backed man in dust-covered clothes separated from the working men. His eyes appraised Real and Finn as if they'd looked at many men in the past. Real judged the man's bearing as military.

'Gentlemen?' the man said.

'I'm Real Lee. This is Finn McBride. We ride together betimes.'

'Betimes?'

'Yeah. I learned that word at Virginia Military Institute.'

47

The man gave Real a sharp look. 'I'm Walter Lambert,' he said. 'These men and I are with the Assembly of Christ.'

'Considering that Eli Jackson's place got burned down a couple of days ago, I'd think a man of your background would have pickets out. Never can tell who'll come riding up.'

Lambert looked embarrassed. 'You're correct, of course. I'll see to it.'

Real grinned. 'Major? Colonel?'

Lambert took a deep breath. 'Not that it's any of your affair, but yes, I was a major. Army Corps of Engineers.'

'Hmm. Good man to build a dam. I reckon it will hold once you get it in.'

'It will.'

Finn McBride spoke. 'Looks to me like you're taking the hard way. You're gonna knock down those spires and use the rock for your dam, right?'

'Yes. Though it may take some time.'

'A lot longer than the middle of next week, I reckon.'

'Look. I don't have time to stand here exchanging pleasantries with you gentlemen. Could you state your business and let me get back to more important things?'

Real exchanged glances with Finn. 'Well,' he said, 'Arthur Whiting hired us to kind of watch over the Assembly. Protect you all, you might say.'

'Who's Arthur Whiting?'

'He owns the biggest spread in north Texas, and he's Angela Freelock's daddy.'

'May I return to my work?' Lambert seemed upset at the mention of Angela Freelock.

'Kinda doing it the hard way, ain't you?' Finn asked.

'Look, McBride. I do with what I've got. If I had blasting powder, we'd have the spires down in a day. I have none, so we do it the hard way, as you mention. If you have a better idea, I'd be pleased to hear it.'

Finn turned and dug into one of his bulging saddle-bags. He withdrew a stick of dynamite. 'Never can tell when a stick or two of this stuff will come in handy,' he said.

Lambert's eyes fastened on the explosive. Then he looked crestfallen. 'Don't tease me, McBride,' he said. 'We've nothing to pay for your dynamite. It's as good as useless to me.'

Finn looked over at Real. 'Did you hear any talk about money?'

'Nope.'

'Then what say you go keep an eye out, and me and the major will blow down some rock towers. That suit you, Major?'

Lightning, Sparrow, and the cowboy Rolly Grieves sat their horses at the edge of the hogback where they could over-look the Assembly village. The cabins occupied a central square that looked like it was laid out to be a town, if anyone else ever joined the church.

'Where you reckon she is, Rolly?'

Rolly Grieves thought about the problem for a moment. 'I ain't never met with her in broad daylight before,' he said.

'You recognize her from far off?'

'I reckon.'

'See anyone that looks like her out there right now?'

Rolly shook his head.

'How do you let her know when you're around?' Lightning sounded worldly, but he'd never had a girl,

49

and he was interested in finding out how such things worked.

'See that old Ponderosa on the far side, over by that clay bank?'

'Yeah.'

'I put pebbles in a woodpecker hole in that old tree. White pebble means I'll be at the tree when the sun sets. Dark pebble means I went by but couldn't stop.'

'You with them that burned the churchman's house?' Sparrow spoke with an accent.

Rolly looked at the ground. 'Told Ace I'd rather not burn good folks outta house and home,' he said. 'Ace didn't say nothing, and he left me behind to "watch things," he said.'

'We'd better put a dark pebble in that tree,' Lightning said. 'It's some ride to the Cibie and we want to look around twixt here and there. You want to do it Rolly, or should me or Sparrow?'

'I'll do it.'

'We'll wait here, then. You stay out of sight, too, if you can.'

'I'll keep to the junipers,' Rolly said. 'Done it afore.'

'Ride, then. Be back by noon or so.'

Rolly rode off, angling northwest, keeping stands of juniper between himself and the Assembly town.

'He don't do too bad for a young'un,' Lightning said, 'but he needs a good teacher. How about you, Sparrow?'

'No time. Got horses to train back at the Flying W.'

Lightning laughed. 'You lucky sumbitch. You got some-place to go back to and something to do when you get there. Shit.'

'The Wolf Wilder teaches me what he knows. I cannot leave until I learn it all.'

'Come on. Let's have a look around,' Lightning said, and reined his horse off down the hill.

Rolly sat his bay horse behind a clump of pinons when Sparrow and Lightning returned to the hogback.

'Get your pebble in the hole?' Lightning asked.

'Yeah.' Rolly didn't sound satisfied. 'Don't like leaving without seeing her.'

'Sometimes we gotta do things we don't like. Make up for it later.' Lightning sounded philosophical for an almost sixteen-year-old who'd never had a girl.

'She got her house burned down, Lightning. Ace and them done it. Cibie riders and them gunhands done it.'

'Gunhands?'

'Mr Brockman sent Ace to Big Johney Gulch to hire gunhands. He come back with Pearson Tate, Amos Dwyer, Tag Eidelbaur, and some others.'

Lightning's face lit up. 'Tag Eidelbaur. Now that's interesting. Real interesting.'

Sparrow spoke. 'How many head on Cibie range?'

'Ace always says ten thousand.'

'Lots of cows.' Sparrow stared at Rolly.

'Yeah.'

'Then why don't we see so many?' Sparrow's face was solemn.

Rolly looked from Sparrow to Lightning and back again. 'Ain't never thought much about it,' he said.

'Come on,' Lightning said. 'We got to get you back to the Cibie. Won't do for you to go missing, Rol.'

'I reckon.' Rolly gazed at the Assembly village, a longing look on his face. 'Hope she gets my pebble.'

'She ever missed before?'

'Nope.'

'Don't worry, then,' Lightning said. He turned Patches

51

south. 'Better we move along.'

'Ten thousand,' Sparrow said. 'Many, many.'

'Heard tell there's an outfit moving on to the plateau from Texas,' Lightning said. 'They're bringing more'n fifty thousand. Outfit's called the Hashknife. Grass is belly high to a tall horse right now. Don't know what all those cows will do to it, though.'

Sparrow gigged his grey mare off to the east toward a long draw that led off up toward the rim country a dozen or more miles away.

'We follow him?' Rolly asked.

'Nah. He'll be along,' Lightning said. 'Sure don't see any sign of Cibie cows, Rol. Wherebouts you figure they are?'

'Hard to tell. Sometimes they stray all the way to Bear Flat and up to See Canyon.'

'You must have a bunch of hands looking after all that beef.'

Rolly rode on, staring at the ground. He looked up. 'That's just it,' he said finally. 'Since Mr Brockman had that horse fall on him, hands've been leaving. Right now, there's only me, Pissant Kilburn, Snakehead Turley, Jesus Baca, and the *segundo*, Ace Duggan.'

'Five hands to herd ten thousand cows?'

'We'll get help for roundup.'

'Shee-it,' Lightning said, echoing Real's favorite expression.

The clatter of iron horseshoes on rock broke into their conversation. Lightning put a hand on the butt of his Remington. Sparrow charged over an eyebrow hill and came at them on the run.

Lightning pulled his new Winchester from its scabbard and levered a bullet into the chamber. Rolly looked too scared to even reach for the old Colt at his belt.

Sparrow's gray mare slammed to a stop on stiff forelegs. 'Somebody drives many cows,' Sparrow said. 'That way.' He pointed northeast, away from Cibie.

6

Real Lee sat with his back to a sandstone outcrop. A screen
of scrawny pinons hid him from the casual eye. A hollow
boom from where Major Lambert and his gaggle of God-
botheres were quarrying rock for their dam sounded like
cannon fire, and took Real back to that day in May when
the cadet corps of VMI faced blue-coated Union troops
outside New Market in the Shenandoah Valley.

Lee's mind went back to the time two days past his fif-
teenth birthday when he was a Rat. He and the rest of the
Rat mass had yet to go through breakout, to earn the rank
of Cadet Private. But being a Rat and being from one of
Virginia's old families earned him the undivided attention
and unfeigned scorn of Benford Seffleck, Class of '66 and
Dyke to Real Lee.

A long drum roll called general quarters in the dark of
night. Before Real could roll from his hay, the toe of
Seffleck's boot caught him in the ribs. He scrambled to his
feet and strained to attention, chin on collarbone.

'Shitsucking Rat. Can't you hear that drum? Asshole.
Bird turd. General quarters! Get your hairless ass to the
parade ground. You've got two minutes.'

'Yessir, Dyke sir.' Real shouted as if Seffleck were fifty

54

yards away.

'Two minutes,' Seffleck screamed. 'Get to it.'

Real pulled his uniform pants from under his hay, the straw-filled pad he used as a bed. His weight had pressed them so sharp creases showed down the legs. He scrambled into them while struggling to put on his blouse and uniform coat. He shoved his stockinged feet into his boots, crammed on a kepi, and ran for the parade ground, buttoning blouse and coat as he went.

He strained to attention in his place between Sam Naylor and Bill Cocke, fellow Rats. In seconds, Seffleck shoved his face into Real's. 'Rat Lee,' he shouted, spraying Real with spittle. 'Do you call this a clean uniform?' Seffleck wiped muddy hands on Real's uniform coat, streaking it with wet clay.

'Seffleck.'

'Yes, sir.' Seffleck turned.

'Tonight's not the night to haze the Rats. Leave it be.'

Yes, sir, First Sergeant Cadell,' Seffleck said.

'I'll get your ass, Rat,' he said when Cadell had moved on. 'Just like I'll get his.'

Seffleck took his place in the ranks, a row behind the Rats.

Two hundred and sixty-five cadets stood in iron rod-straight lines. Commandant Lieutenant Colonel Shipp's eyes swept their ranks. 'Gentlemen,' he said, 'your country calls. We are to meet General Breckinridge's army at Staunton on the morrow. You will draw ammunition, clean your pieces, sharpen your bayonets, and fall in here at dawn.'

The adjutant barked, 'Dismissed.'

On 11 May, 1864, the cadets marched from Lexington,

Virginia. They carried new Lorenz rifle muskets, 40 rounds in ammunition pouches, bayonets in scabbards, full marching haversacks with two days' rations, two blankets, ground cloths, and canteens. They covered the eighty-one miles to New Market in four days, most of the distance in pouring rain.

May 15 came overcast and dark and the skies still drizzled. Real Lee lined up in ranks with the Rat mass of Company D. Cadet First Sergeant Bill Cadell paced the formation, making sure the Rats stood firm and upheld the honor of VMI Cadets. Seffleck was somewhere behind. Real couldn't see him, but felt the Dyke's malevolent presence.

General Breckinridge rode across the field in front of the corps. 'Gentlemen,' he shouted, 'I know you will do your duty!' Real struggled to stand straighter and taller, his stomach in a knot.

The order to move forward came at noon. Wind whipped the heavy rain.

'Cadets, we are at the center of the line,' shouted Colonel Shipp. 'On your honor! Fix bayonets. Company A to the left. Company D to the right. In line of skirmishers, march!'

Real moved to his position in the line. Before he could move, a Union shell exploded and knocked down the colonel and his gray horse. Both lay bloody and motionless. Real swallowed hard, and stared straight ahead. His insides trembled. He let out a yell, so his fellow Rats wouldn't know he was scared. He scanned the company for Seffleck and saw him at the very end of the skirmish line, his face turned away.

'Forward,' bellowed Cadell.

Union guns barked. To Real's left, Chuck Crockett fell,

56

his face a bloody mask. Real stepped around the downed cadet. He couldn't stop to help; he had to move on. He ground his teeth in frustration.

'Close up those lines,' Cadell roared.

Real sidestepped until Crockett's place was filled.

The cadets moved forward, splitting to go around a farmhouse. They plunged into a brush-studded ravine. Real ducked below the ravine bank. Canister and grapeshot snapped overhead. For the moment he was out of the line of fire. He didn't remember pulling the trigger, but his gun was empty. He panted and reloaded. Where was Seffleck? Again Real quickly looked around. Seffleck lagged at least three steps behind. He saw Real glance at him and screwed up his face in a fierce stare.

'Cadets. Forward,' Cadell shouted.

The corps scrambled up out of the ravine, emerging before Breckinridge's veteran army. Real glanced sideways at the regulars. To his amazement, officers had to threaten soldiers with their pistols to get them to charge the Union troops. He lifted his head. VMI cadets, even Rats, would do their duty. It was part of their code of honor.

The rain fell, and still the guns fired.

Real's Lorenz rifle musket had been issued to him only two days before his country's call. Still, he'd practiced long and hard with his Cadet Musket 1841, and the two guns were similar. The Lorenz's barrel reached 37½ inches toward the target, and shot a .54 caliber bullet, slotted so it would expand into the riflings and spin, which greatly improved its accuracy. Real's Lorenz bore the stamp 863, made in 1863, only a year before. He felt a flash of pride. A VMI Rat, just turned fifteen, and he held a brand-new rifle musket, made in Austria, to use against the bluebellies.

The cadets started across a fresh-plowed wheat field. Rain poured down. Yankee cannons boomed. Real kept his Lorenz ready, cap on nipple, but he saw no Yankees to shoot.

The sticky mud sucked at Real's boots. He lost one. Then the other. Then his socks. The Lorez was capped and ready. Barefooted, he pushed on, not even taking the time to look around for Seffleck.

Brush at the edge of the field hid them from the Yankees, as did a dilapidated rail fence. 'Forward,' Captain Wise yelled, and the corps scrambled over the fence in the face of Yankee grape shot and marched on. Steadily, they moved toward the heights.

Cadet Sergeant Cadell went down. Real knew when he passed him that Cadell was dead. He had a bullet hole in the back of his head. A flash of anger surged through his breast as he searched for a blue-clad target. He could see the Yankee battery now. They shoved bags of powder down the muzzle without swabbing out. Real dropped to one knee. The Lorenz was sighted in for a hundred yards. The battery was beyond that. Real held high and touched off the Lorenz. It kicked his shoulder and sent the 250-grain bullet on its way. Through the powder smoke, Real saw the Union soldier throw his hands wide and fall. He felt grimly satisfied and a little chagrined. As a CSA soldier, he'd done his duty. As a man, he'd shot another human. He stood and began reloading the Lorenz as he marched ahead.

Yankee cannons fired canister and grape shot. Cadets fell like broken dolls. Their comrades closed up ranks. VMI moved forward.

'Charge. Charge. Charge!' The cry went up and down the cadet line. Real fired the Lorenz again, then moved forward and upward at a trot, the rifle held at port arms, bayonet thrusting into the air. Seffleck was the least of his worries.

The Union troops fell back. Real screamed his Rebel yell. Horses hastily hitched to caissons and cannons lunged against their harnesses and four of the six Yankee cannons lumbered away toward the bridge below Rude's Hill.

Without realizing he was in the van, Real topped the hill with Bill Cocke half a step behind. Cocke fired, and a Union soldier fell. Smoke rose from the .54 hole in his blue tunic.

An officer lay with one leg under his dead horse. As Real charged toward him, the Yankee struggled to get his pistol from its flapped holster. Real came to a stop in front of the officer, his bayonet inches from the man's chest. 'The day is lost for you, sir,' he said. 'Best you surrender so our surgeons can tend to your injuries.'

'Shit,' the Yankee said, dropping the revolver. 'Tend to my injuries my ass. You all will just send me to Andersonville.'

'That could be,' Real said, 'but at least you're alive.'

'Shit. Beat by a bunch of boys. Who are you, youngster?'

Real snapped to a Rat's strained attention posture. 'Cadet Private Gabriel Winston Lee,' he said. 'Virginia Military Institute.'

'Carlton Riess,' the officer replied. 'Can you get this damned horse off my leg?'

Cadet Color Sergeant Evans waved the VMI flag from atop a caisson, while the cadets cheered. Real couldn't see Seffleck anywhere, and when cadet roll call was taken, he was missing.

Another blast sounded, followed by the rumble of a sandstone spire collapsing into pieces. The sound of an explosion brought Real back to Green Valley. 'Yeah, we pushed the Yankees out of Shenandoah Valley,' he muttered, 'then they came and burned VMI. Some revenge.'

Memories of the bloody day at New Market didn't keep Real Lee's eyes from continually sweeping the country. He saw the riders as soon as they broke through the willows along Little Green Valley Creek. Real shucked his Colt and fired three shots into the air. He holstered the six-gun, stood up as if nothing in the world bothered him, ambled over to the outcrop where Sorry browsed on chamise, and mounted the bright red sorrel.

'Come on, Sorry,' he said. 'We've got company.' He pulled the 10-gauge Ithaca from its scabbard under the onside stirrup leather and checked its loads. Double-aught buckshot. He dug four more shells from the offside saddle-bag and dropped them into his shirt pocket.

The riders had reined up when Real fired his warning shots, but now rode forward again, long guns held upright, butts on thighs.

Real figured the riders were a show of force, but there was no way to be sure. Still, he had to take the chance. Major Lambert and the God-botherers had no weapons. Real had to turn the gunmen back.

The trail from the creek to the sandstone spires narrowed about a mile on, with a low ridge on one side and a rolling hogback on the other. Real met the riders halfway through.

The leader held up his hand and the others reined in. They sat nonchalant in their saddles as Real approached.

'That's close enough, Real Lee,' the man said.

Real lowered the Ithaca but left both hammers cocked. 'Well, well, Pearson Tate. Who'd've expected you this far away from a faro table?'

60

He nodded at the two gunmen who flanked Tate. 'Tag. Amos.'

'Didn't know you were involved in this fracas, Real,' Tate said.

'I am. What brings such as you to this neck of the woods?'

'Gun work.'

'Can't let you go any farther, Pearson. You and your gunnies better pull out of Green Valley before someone gets killed.'

Pearson Tate laughed.

Real shifted the Ithaca's twin barrels in Tate's direction. 'You know me, Pearson. I don't bluff.' He raised his voice. 'You there, Finn?'

'I am.' Finn McBride's voice came from a jumble of large rocks that had broken away from the ridge in eons past.

'Pearson, I'd like your men to meet Finn McBride. He's bashful, so he'll likely not come out for formal introductions, but know this. Finn's very familiar with dynamite, and he always carries a few sticks. So here's how it stands.'

Real used his left hand to shove his Stetson back on his head. 'One of you makes a move, and I kill Pearson Tate. When Finn hears my Ithaca go off, he lights a stick of dynamite and a couple of seconds later, half a dozen or so of you all will be pushing up sunflowers. That sound fair?'

Tag Eidelbaur, a slight man in a bowler hat and four-button coat, sat on a big horse. His right cheek ticked as he squinted at Real Lee.

Real grinned.

'Chances are he's bluffing, Tate,' Eidelbaur said.

'You all know Gus Snyder? Real asked. 'He hired out a dozen riders to Robert Dunn in Ponderosa to clean Finn

McBride and his woman off the Rafter P at Paradise Valley. They rode up to the Rafter P big as you please. Finn and Laurel blasted them away. Robert Dunn and a bunch of Gus's riders died.'

A bearded man in the back of the group of riders spoke up. 'Boss, I heard about that. Shotgun Lou Grimes said luck was the only way he got out alive.'

'Take a hint, Pearson,' Real said. 'Leave Green Valley.'

Tate sat quietly on his big palomino for a long moment. Then he said, 'You've got the upper hand, Real. We'll back off for now. But there are only two of you. We'll settle this when the time's right.'

Real laughed out loud. 'You'd better count your chickens, Pearson Tate. Me and Finn, we're only half. Tangle with us and you tangle with Tom Easter and Wolf Wilder, and a couple of youngsters that're tagging along. Lightning Brewster's the fastest man I ever saw draw a Colt .45, and something makes me think Jaime Sparrow's full-blooded Apache. Lot more'n two, Pearson. A lot more.'

'We'll soon own this valley, Real, lock, stock, and barrel.'

'Ain't gonna happen. The Assembly's legal and this dam is a viable improvement. The range is full of Cibie cows. Can't see you taking over, but you're welcome to try. Now. Are you leaving, or do Finn and I have to blow you all to hell?'

Tate remained silent for another long moment, chewing on his lip in frustration.

'You got that cigarillo lit, Finn?'

'Lit and puffing, Real. You just say when.'

'God damn you, Real Lee. God damn you to hell.' Tate started to rein his palomino around.'

'Pearson,' Real called. 'Who's behind this grab? You

all're not what Cyril Brockman bargained for. I'll just bet you're not. Who's behind it?'

This time Tate laughed. 'Don't you wish you knew?' He turned the palomino and led the gunnies back down the trail toward Little Green Valley Creek.

Finn McBride stepped out from behind the screen of fallen rock. 'Good riddance,' he said. 'Glad I didn't have to use any of this.' He held up a stick of dynamite. 'Need it all to blow them spires down.'

Real watched the gunmen disappear into the willow screen along the creek. 'We'll have it to do sometime, Finn. Pearson Tate's not one to give up. And someone behind him is pushing mighty hard. We'll have plenty of gun work to do before it's all over.'

7

The man called Kyle Benford sat at his customary table in the Branding Iron saloon on Overland Street in Payson. In the morning hours, there were only two serious drinkers at the Branding Iron bar. The girls were still asleep in their rooms and would be until the free lunch customers had gone.

Benford smiled to himself. The Branding Iron had done well for him and he was about to close a deal that would put him among the high rollers in Arizona: a governorship might well be the result. His smile widened.

Pearson Tate would soon bring news of progress. The people known as the Assembly of Christ would be on their way to parts unknown, and Benford's men could then pick the Cibie clean before taking over the entire Green Valley.

An unseasonal rain fell on Payson, gradually turning the streets into deepening mire. Benford couldn't care less. He had no reason to go outside the Branding Iron. He lifted a carefully polished boot to the chair beside him and pulled a 3-inch cheroot from the inner pocket of his pearl gray coat. He lit the smoke with a lucifer he scratched into flame on the underside of the table. A haze of blue smoke soon hung around Benford's head. God, but life was good.

Pearson Tate came through the back door in mid-afternoon. 'Can the boys come in, Boss?' he asked Benford. 'The long ride from Green Valley's made them thirsty.'

Benford waved his assent and Tate shouted out the door. 'In. First drink's on me. House whiskey or beer. After that, you're on your own.'

Riders crowded through the door, dripping water and tracking mud on to the sawdust that covered the floor. A rough bunch, but Benford knew they were ready to do a job and the money they spent in the Branding Iron was the same color as the cash of any hoity-toity from the other side of Beeline.

Tate brought a bottle of Old Quaker rye to Benford's table. He poured three fingers and downed the whiskey in a single gulp.

'Do you have a problem?' Benford said.

Tate shook his head. 'Nothing we can't handle.'

Benford showed an icy smile. 'Why don't you let me be the judge of that, Tate. Tell me what happened. Did you move the pumpkin rollers out?'

'They've got gunmen guarding them.'

'Gunmen?'

'Gunmen.'

'Who?'

'The names I heard were Tom Easter, Wolf Wilder, a dynamite thrower by the name of Finn McBride, a couple of youngsters, and. . . .'

Benford leaned forward.

'. . . they've got Real Lee out front.'

Benford sat back in his chair. He thought for a long moment. 'Real Lee,' he said, almost to himself. He straightened up. 'I don't care how you do it, Tate, but bring me Real Lee.'

'Mr Lee?' The youngster stood with his floppy hat held in both hands.

Real grinned. 'What is it, kid?!'

'Brother Richards, he's the elder in charge, Brother Richards told me to invite Mr Lee and Mr McBride to share our evening meal. "Mr Lee brung in the venison we're having, and it just seems right," Brother Richards said.' The youngster held back and looked at Real and Finn sideways, like they might have some kind of catching disease.

'What do you think, Finn?' Real asked.

'No harm, I reckon. I'm tired of cooking for you and me anyway.'

'We'll be over to your fire 'fore long, youngster,' Real said. 'How about you tell us your name?'

'Loran Richards, Mr Lee,' the boy said.

'So Brother Richards is your Pa?' Real asked.

'Nah. Oldest brother. Pa's dead.' The boy scraped at the dirt with the toe of his shoe. 'Ma's dead, too. Just me and Rod and Lou Jean,' he said, his voice little more than a whisper.

'Your brother must be some kind of man, then,' Real said. 'Him being leader and all.'

'He's got faith,' the boy said. 'I gotta go. I'll tell him you're coming over.' He sprinted away.

'Kid left in a hurry,' Real said.

'Didn't want to catch any of your heathen ways, I reckon,' Finn said and grinned. 'Let's go and see how those god-botherers fixed that venison you shot.'

'Lead the way.'

Finn scraped dirt on to their little coffee fire with the

66

sole of his boot. 'Don't want no grass fires,' he said. He poured the remaining coffee on the fire to finish the job. 'OK. Let's go.'

The walk wasn't much more than a hundred yards, but Real and Finn took it slow. Even if the bible-thumpers had no weapons, it wasn't a good idea to go walking up on a fire like the whole world was calm and friendly.

'Hello, the fire,' Real called out when they got close enough. 'Two friendly men with bellies that think their throats have been cut are coming in.'

'Welcome to you,' a voice said. The fragrance of venison and sliced onions, cooked in deep Dutch ovens, filled the camp.

'Someone knows what to do with dead deer,' Real said. 'Mighty glad for the invite.'

'God sent you to protect us, Mr Lee,' said a sturdy young man. He thrust out his hand. 'I'm Evan Richards,' he said. 'Pastor Jackson put me in charge of the dam-building group, though Brother Lambert is to show us how it is done.'

Real Lee grasped the young man's hand. 'Met your younger brother earlier. Seems like a good lad.'

Richards smiled. 'Thank you. It's been hard on him since our parents passed on.'

'The venison smells mighty good, Richards. Glad to help you get rid of it.'

Real lifted the lid of a Dutch oven and took a deep breath of the steam that rose from the cast-iron pot. 'Almighty good, I'd say.'

The Assemblymen raked baked potatoes from the fire and put one on each tin plate, then Richards added a slice of fried venison and some onions. The first plates were handed to Real and Finn. Real was about to jab his fork into the meat when Richards said,

'We say grace in our camp, Mr Lee. If you could fore-bear for a moment until everyone gets their food. . . .'

'Oh,' Real said. 'Yeah.'

Finn grinned at Real's discomfort. 'Time you got some religion anyway, Real. You been a heathen too long.'

'I saw what religion does to people when I was in the Legion,' he said. 'Makes fanatics out of simple men.'

'Legion?' Richards asked.

Real turned haunted eyes on the young Assemblyman. 'No room in the Army for many VMI grads, Class of '70, so I joined the French Foreign Legion. Want to see what religion can do to a man? Go to Africa, or Indochina. You'll learn.' He turned his attention to his plate. 'We ever going to eat this dead deer?' he asked.

Richards looked around. 'Brother Smithson, please,' he said.

The Assemblymen all took their hats off and bowed their heads.

A short man with shoulders like a giant stepped forward. 'Dear Lord,' he said. 'We thank Thee for Thy bounty and for Thy blessings upon us this day. May this food give us the strength to do Thy will in Christ's name. Amen.'

'Amen,' the others chorused, and plunged into their food as if they'd not eaten in three days.

The meat was excellent: covered in flour and fried in bacon grease. The onions had picked up a taste of venison as the venison had been seasoned by the onions. And a touch of salt added to the flavor.

'Damn,' Real said. 'This meat is right good.'

'Please, Mr Lee. There is no need to be profane,' Richards said.

'Oh. Yeah. Sorry.' Real didn't look up from his plate until all the food, including a very large baked potato, was gone.

'Would you like a cup of coffee, Mr Lee,' asked Loran Richards.

'I'd admire one, Loran,' Real said. 'Nothing better than sitting around the fire talking with friends over well-brewed coffee.'

'Are we your friends, Mr Lee?'

'I'd like to think so. I'm friendly to anyone who's friendly to me.' Real gave the boy his biggest smile. 'Now you go on and give the others some of that Arbuckles.' He sat on one of the big rocks the Assembly had brought to the fire to serve as seats. He took a sip of the coffee and wished he hadn't. Not a hint of Arbuckles anywhere. He'd tasted better coffee made from chicory at VMI. He had to struggle not to spit it out on the ground. His face must have said something.

'Something wrong, Mr Lee?' Hugh Freelock asked.

Real shook his head, and ventured another sip. It was just as bad, but Real was able to swallow without changing expression. 'Never had coffee like this before,' he said.

'We make our own,' Freelock said, 'with acorns. After a while, it's not bad.'

'Take some getting used to, I reckon.' Real took another sip.

'Well, Brothers Richards and Lambert, we'll knock that final spire down tomorrow,' Finn McBride said, 'then me and Real will get outta your hair.'

'You're no bother,' Lambert said. 'Those men would have run us over had you not been here.'

'They'll be back,' Real said.

Lambert said nothing, and the Assemblymen stared at

the ground. No one seemed willing to broach the subject of what would happen when Pearson Tate and his men returned.

'They'll be back,' Real said again, 'and there's a chance we won't be here to protect you.'

'God will protect us,' Richards said, but his voice lacked conviction.

'That's interesting,' Real said. 'We had us a chaplain at VMI where I went to school. He used to quote Ben Franklin's Poor Richard's Almanac. I kinda like old Ben's idea. He said, 'God helps them who help themselves.' I reckon that's the way the real world works.'

'Jesus Christ said the meek would inherit the Earth,' Richards said. 'We believe in being meek, and we believe that means not bearing arms for any purpose, though we may lose our lives.'

'How much of the Earth have you inherited so far?' Real's question carried a barb.

'You lay off my brother,' Loran Richards said. 'He's got faith, and it ain't good for you to go about destroying it. It's his faith. Not yours. You believe what you want, but let my brother believe what he wants, too.'

Real was silent for a long moment. 'Sorry, Richards,' he said at last. 'I wasn't trying to make you out as mistaken. I just hoped you'd see how things are here in Arizona right now.' He turned to young Loran. 'You're right to stick up for your brother, boy. I was wrong. All wrong. I'm sorry.

'Finn, I figure you and I'd better get on back to camp. Morning will come early enough,' Real said. He tossed the acorn coffee away and handed the cup to Loran. 'Thanks, boy. Take care,' he said, and walked away.

The brethren had only four wagons, and none would carry

the six tons of a Murphy. But Walt Lambert kept them rolling steadily between the fallen spires and the dam site. The sandstone the wagons dumped would form a line across the stream, bowing slightly into the current. As the men toppled boulders into the places Lambert said they should go, Loran and another boy trundled wheelbarrows full of dirt to pack into the cracks between the rocks, locking them in place.

Real Lee and Walt Lambert stood on high ground where Lambert could oversee work on the dam.

'Looks like you all have got things lined out,' Real said. 'Reckon it's time for me and Finn to head back to your town . . . you got a name for that burg yet?'

Lambert watched work on the dam through a pair of field glasses. 'Our town?' he said. 'Pastor Jackson says it's Respite.'

'Respite, eh? Hope that's what you get. It's been a wild country, but I figure maybe we're growing out of it. Maybe you all can help civilize Arizona.'

Lambert gave Real a thin smile. 'If we don't get annihilated first.'

'There's that,' Real said. 'Pearson Tate's not a man to take on lightly.' Real took a deep breath. 'Walt, I don't know where they'll hit, here or Respite, but they'll hit. You were in the Army. Can't imagine you not protecting yourself.'

Lambert turned to stare at Real. Then he nodded. 'I've got a Sharps and a Single Action Army. I keep them out of sight.'

'Got bullets for them?'

'Forty for the Sharps, about the same for the SAA.'

'Hmmm. I understand you keeping your weapons out of sight,' Real said, 'but I reckon you'd better keep them

71

close to hand. If Tate and his men start harassing you, you'll have to bring them out into plain sight. You ready for that?'

'I'll do what I have to do.'

'Yeah. A man tends to do that.'

'Me and Finn need to go back to our camp above Respite. You're an Army man, you know what to do. Pickets, and a fast horse to come to us if trouble shows.'

'These people really believe the meek will inherit the Earth?' Lambert asked.

'Yeah.'

'I'll do what I can.'

'Look. If the Assembly gets a foothold, you'll make a good town. One where kids can grow up without their stomachs all screwed up in knots 'cause they're scared. I've seen bad places in my time. This ain't one of them. Build your dam, Walt Lambert, build your town, and build good lives for yourselves and your families.'

They watched the wagons come and go. 'We'll be moving along,' Real said, and walked to where Sorry was ground-tied. He tightened the surcingle, climbed aboard, and waved a hand at Lambert.

'I hate to leave right now, but we're packed and ready. Let's go, Sorry.' The sorrel moved out as if he understood every word Real Lee said.

Real turned to Finn McBride, who rode beside him. 'I do feel a bit better,' he said. 'At least Walt Lambert's got guns.'

8

Real and Finn McBride rode into camp near sundown. Tom Easter and Wolf Wilder were there, but not the youngsters. The place had taken on the look of a semi-permanent camp with a wickiup and a lean-to, and a picket line for the horses.

'Looks right to home,' Real said.

'Wonder how the grub is?' Finn said.

'Always worried about what's going into your stomach, Finn. Always worried about that, ain't you?' Real laughed.

'You've got no idea how much I'm sacrificing, Real. Laurel's simply the best cook this side of San Francisco, and maybe all the way to the Sandwich Islands. Going without her cooking is a serious hardship.' Finn heaved a sigh. 'Sure hankering to go home,' he said.

Real Lee made no reply. Who was he to make light of such comments? He had nothing but a good sorrel horse to carry him and reliable weapons that worked when he needed them. He was never in a place long enough to form an attachment beyond a fling with one of the doves in whichever saloon he staked out as his current place of residence, except for Lilywhite, that is. 'A good thing, that,' he said, 'coming home to a warm fire and a good cup of coffee in a house you built with your own hands. You've got a good thing, Finn. A good thing.'

'You can say that again,' Finn said. 'Cuts a man's wandering down to nothing, real quick.'

'Damn,' Real said.

Finn gave him a very self-satisfied smile. 'Nah. It ain't Hell, neither, though it came close for a while there.'

'You and yours did good in that fight, Finn. Sometimes all a man can do is get his back up and fight like a wounded grizzly to protect what's his.' Real's voice held a touch of bitterness.

Finn said no more.

Tom Easter stood from where he'd been hunkered down by the fire. 'Dam going OK?'

'Lambert's a good engineer,' Real said. 'Had a bit of trouble with Pearson Tate and a bunch of gunnies, but Finn scared 'em off.' Real grinned, then went serious. 'Tate'll be back, I reckon. There's something bigger going on here than running off a bunch of pumpkin rollers.'

Real dismounted and started to unsaddle Sorry. 'What'd Brockman have to say, Tom?' he asked.

Easter shook his head. 'Brockman's got a pet Chinaman that keeps him smoked up on opium. Didn't make much sense when we talked to him.'

'Hands?'

'Ace Duggan, the segundo, is running things as best he can, but Brockman's ordered him to run the Assembly off. Told him to get help from Tom Ranklin at Big Johney Gulch. Ace talked to Ranklin, and next thing, Pearson Tate showed up, offering to help. Ace says he ain't paid Tate a dime. Also says the Cibie is missing cattle, lots of cattle.'

'Hands?' Real repeated.

Easter gave him a hard look. 'Two men and a boy,' he said. 'That's all.'

'She-it.' Real dumped his gear on a flat spot at the far side of the fire, and pulled a tin cup from its thong on the saddle. He filled the cup from the big pot at the edge of the fire. Finn McBride joined him. Wolf Wilder sat stolid in front of the wickiup, eyes closed.

A twig snapped and Real put a hand to the butt of his '78 Colt Police. Sparrow stepped around the wickiup.

'Lots of noise for someone like you, Sparrow,' Real said.

Sparrow's lips twitched in what may have been the start of a smile. 'Wouldn't want to sneak up on you all, Mr Lee,' he said.

Wilder opened his eyes and looked a question at Sparrow.

'We found a big herd of Cibie cows,' Sparrow said. 'They're bunched up in a box canyon off Bull Tank. Ain't all that much grass in there. They won't stay put long. Lightning stayed there to keep an eye on them.'

'How many?'

'Four.'

'No. How many cows?' Real asked.

'The canyon's full of them,' Sparrow said.

'Only two reasons to rustle another man's cows,' Real said. 'One is to get a start herd for a new operation, the other's money.'

'May be neither,' Tom Easter said. 'Holding cows off the range might be a way of caving a ranch in.'

'We're here to watch over the Assembly,' Finn said. 'Can't start chasing cows for the Cibie.'

'Brockman's out of it,' Easter said. 'I'd say someone's moving in on Cibie range.'

'So what's in it for us? Whiting hired us to watch out for

his daughter, not the Cibie.' Real put a hand to his face and scrubbed his fingers through the two-day stubble. 'When Pearson Tate came to see what the dam-builders were doing, he said the whole valley would be theirs. The whole valley.'

'Cows and Assembly and Cibie and Tate's gaggle of gunmen. They're all in the same pot, then,' Easter said.

'I'll fix supper,' Finn said. 'Sun's down, and a man thinks better when his stomach's not growling at him.' He went to the deer haunch hanging from a Ponderosa at the edge of camp and carved slices of the meat into a tin plate. 'Nothing fancy,' he said. 'I'll fry up some venison and make a little frybread to go with it.'

'Wish we knew if Tate's outfit is holding those cows,' Real said. 'That would tie it all together.'

Wolf Wilder said something to Sparrow in a language Real didn't understand, and it wasn't Spanish. The dark young man nodded and slipped off into the darkness. 'Sparrow will find out who guards the cows,' Wilder said.

The smell of frying venison rose from Finn's pan. He kneaded flour and water and a pinch of salt for frybread, which would go into the frying pan when the venison was done. Tom Easter dug out his cleaning gear and went to work on his weapons, first the Winchester and then the Colt. Wolf Wilder still sat cross-legged before the wickiup, arms folded and eyes closed. Everyone looked calm except for Real Lee.

Real fussed with his gear, setting up his sleeping place. He'd soon need a lean-to like Tom's if they were staying long. But the more he thought about it, the less he liked the situation. It felt like trying to grab a handful of fog. Who backed Pearson Tate and those gunnies? Who wanted Green Valley, and why?

'This meat's as close to done as it'll get,' Finn said, 'and the fry bread is in the pan.'

Easter and Wilder dug tin plates from their gear and went to stand over Finn McBride like vultures waiting for a downed cow to die.

'Get your own meat,' Finn said, waving at the pile of venison steaming on a plate near the fire.

Easter stabbed a slice with his Bowie and Wilder used a strange-looking knife he called a kukri. 'Comes from some place called Assam,' he said. 'Got it in Wickenburg.'

Finn forked hunks of fry bread on to their plates. 'Real. You not hungry?'

'Be there in a minute.' Real had a pair of field glasses trained on the Assembly town Jackson called Respite. The communal cooking fire looked within an hour of dying. Two women cleaned up around it. The rest of the town had returned to their cabins. Real wondered where the Jacksons stayed, now that their cabin lay in ashes. He shoved the glasses back into their case. He got a plate and went to get some of Finn McBride's good cooking. 'You ever open an eating place,' he said over a mouthful of venison, 'you've got one steady customer. You could make porcupine taste good, I swear.'

Finn grinned. 'You think I'm a good cook, you should try Charlie Stark's place in Ponderosa.'

'I've eaten in high-collar places from here to Charleston and Paris, France, Finn. But none of those cooks did it over an open fire in the middle of Green Valley.'

Conversation lagged as the four horsemen chewed venison and fry bread, and washed it down with genuine Arbuckle's coffee.

Wilder saw them first. 'Something moving down at the

Assembly,' he said.

Real sprang to his feet and retrieved his field glasses, which he trained on the village.

Dark figures slunk toward the cabins. He could tell they were taking extra care to be silent.

'We'd better warn them,' he said. 'Must be a dozen men down there.' He rushed to the picket line with Sorry's bridle, and slipped it into the sorrel's mouth. He climbed on bareback. 'Come on, Sorry. Let's go do some good.' He gigged the red horse toward Respite. The other three horsemen were still saddling up as Real and Sorry thundered down the hill.

At the bottom of the incline, Real pulled his Colt .45 and fired off three shots as quickly as he could thumb back the hammer. As if the shots were a signal, fires sprang up at the cabins and dark figures ran away from the spreading flames. He was much too far away to have a hope of hitting any of the arsonists, but he fired his remaining bullets at them anyway. The Colt empty, he shoved it back into its holster and drew the Police. Five more bullets. He fired. And fired. And fired again. Shouting, he rode full tilt toward Respite.

Two ropes settled over Real's head, pinned his arms to his side, and jerked him off Sorry's back. Something collided with his head and the world went black.

Real came to face down over Sorry's back, his hands tied to his feet beneath the sorrel's belly. Wherever his attackers were taking him, they went at a trot, and Sorry's jolting gait slammed Real's innards against his backbone. His head hurt. They'd caught him off guard, as if he were a rank tenderfoot. He let his head hang and tried to think of a way out.

78

The horses stopped. Real hung as if he were still uncon-scious. Trail dust filled his nostrils. He breathed through his mouth.

'Dump 'im off that horse,' a voice commanded, and a man untied Real's bindings, then lifted his feet and dumped him on the far side of the horse. He couldn't help grunting when he hit the ground.

'I reckon he's woke up, Boss.' A boot caught Real in the side. 'On your feet, asshole.' A hand took hold of Real's left arm and levered him to his feet. He shook, still unbal-anced from the blow to his head.

Another man grabbed his right arm. The two strong men frogmarched Real through the darkness toward a small fire. They stopped, holding him up between them.

'Gabriel Winston Lee.'

At the sound of his name, Real struggled to raise his head, but couldn't.

A gloved hand smashed into his face. 'I told you, Lee. I told you. I told you when you were a Rat that I'd get you. It's time.' Another slap snapped Real's head sideways. He squinted through the pain, trying to focus on the man in front of him.

'The pride of Virginia can't even stand on his own two feet.'

Real mumbled.

'Can't hear you, Lee!'

Real straightened a little, but mostly the two big men held him up.

'Go . . .'

A fist cut him off, connecting high on his cheekbone. If not for the men holding him, he would have dropped like an ear-shot pig. Another blow caught him at the corner of his mouth, smashing lips and cheek against teeth. He

79

tasted the copper and salt of blood.

'You were saying?'

'G-g-go t' Hell.' Real spoke in a hoarse whisper. He spat blood. Then louder. 'Go straight to Hell.'

A finger beneath his chin lifted Real's face. 'Look at me, Lee. Look at your worst nightmare.'

Real squinted again. He made out a man slightly shorter than his own five-ten. The hard face looked somehow familiar, but who? Blue eyes in deep sockets. Thick eyebrows. Heavy blue of fresh-shaved beard. Thin lips twisted in a sneer. Real shook his head. Looked again. 'Don't know you, shithead,' he managed to say, 'but you're a dead man.'

The man laughed. 'I'm Kyle Benford to you, Lee. We'll see how long it takes you to recognize me.' He slapped Real back and forth across the face. 'Take him to Payson,' Benford said.

9

'You know what I think?' Lightning said to Sparrow.

Sparrow shrugged.

'I think we should put them cows back on Cibie range,' he said.

'How?'

'Only four men keeping them in this canyon. We take them out of the way, we just push the cows out of the canyon. They'll scatter natural.'

Sparrow said nothing. The young men lay atop the canyon rim overlooking the camp that held the Cibie cattle. Whoever was holding the cattle had built a brush wall across the canyon mouth, leaving a space about four cows wide just off center, and the men's campfire guarded the opening.

Patches stamped his foot in irritation because Lightning had tethered him to a scrub oak where he couldn't reach the chamise he loved. The dry dusty smell wafting up and over the canyon rim made Lightning want to sneeze. He stifled the urge.

'Two men at the fire. Two on watch,' Sparrow said. 'You take the man watching this side. Give me an owlhoot. . . .' He stopped for a moment, staring at Lightning. 'You can hoot?' he finally said.

'Can I hoot? Can I hoot? Man, you ain't heard an owl till you've heard me hoot.' His grin was a flash of white teeth in the dark night.

Sparrow pulled his huge Bowie and tested its edge on his thumb. Satisfied, he returned it to the scabbard. 'No guns,' he said.

'Right. No gunshots,' Lightning said. He didn't have a big Bowie knife like Sparrow's.

Sparrow slipped into the night.

Lightning waited. Sparrow needed time to get across the canyon. It felt a lot like the games he played with Inya and Ahwotiga as he was growing up where his pa worked for Alex Rondell at the Dry Springs Trading Post. Hopi and Yavapai and some Navajo people came to the post, and the two Yavapai boys were Lightning's only friends. Funny what a kid can learn just playing around.

Lightning unbuckled his gunbelt and hung it from a scrub oak branch. He shoved the heavy Remington behind his waistband in the small of his back. He didn't want the pistol clicking on rock or digging into the dirt as he slithered up on the sentry. Before slipping off the canyon rim, he sat and listened to the night. Beetles clicked in the jack pine thicket to his left, and a coyote yipped in the dry land across the canyon. Once in a while, a cow lowed from among the hundreds bedded down on the canyon floor. The breeze carried a cool scent from the little stream in the canyon, leavened with the faint smell of cow manure. *Be a nice place to have a homestead*, Lightning thought, then shook the idea away. A drifter like him had no business thinking of homesteads. Real Lee was the kind of man Lightning aimed to be: slick at cards. Slick at gun work. And slick with women. That was how a man should

82

be. Really. Lightning went to where his gunbelt hung in the scrub, pushed a handful of bullets from the loops, and put them in his shirt pocket. He buttoned the flap so he could crawl around without worrying about the bullets falling out. He took a deep breath, and slipped off the edge of the canyon to make his way to the bottom.

Lightning moved carefully toward a piece of high ground topped by a sycamore, the likely place for a night guard. He took his time. A man in a rush made noise.

Lillian Whitehead, better known as Lilywhite, arrived in Payson at the reins of a buggy. The two-year-old town straddled the trail, now a road, from the sheep ranges east of Flagstaff and the cattle country west of the Painted Desert to the meat-eating markets of Globe City, Miami, and the Salt River Valley towns of Mesa and Phoenix. Payson was a growing town, and Lilywhite made money in growing towns.

She first stopped at the Stockman Hotel, where she booked two rooms, one for herself and one for Jorge Valenzuela, son of a Yaqui woman and a Mexican priest, who always rode with her. Lilywhite parked the buggy at Webber's Livery. Jorge took care of the team and his palomino while she waited.

Up Main Street, Lilywhite could see Solomon's Mercantile. Fredrick Solomon ran the store and had a place on the town council, but Lilywhite owned his operation. Solomon provided her with information, and told her of Kyle Benford and his ambitions. Lilywhite smiled at the thought. Nothing more exhilarating than a good business rivalry. After all, she was in Payson to open a new social club called the Swan's Lake.

A new building rose on the corner of Frontier and

Ponderosa. Three stories high, it would house a sophisti-
cated bar, a luxurious lounge, a small theater with stage
and dressing-rooms, places on the second floor for lady
'companions', and a residence on the third floor for
Lilywhite.

Freight wagons with bar mirrors, lounge furniture,
carpets, drapes, chandeliers, and double beds already
moved along the road from Globe City. The interior, with
tongue-and-groove hardwood flooring throughout, would
be finished by the end of the week. Swan's Lake would
open on Monday.

Lilywhite licked her lips. First she'd wash and repair her
make-up. At the entrance of the hotel, she turned to
Jorge, who followed a step and a half behind, always. She
looked at his knife-scarred face. She'd stitched up that
wound and others, and nursed Jorge to health after he
staggered from an alleyway near her lounge in Globe City.
He'd never said where the wounds came from, but he'd
pledged his life to Lilywhite.

'Jorge. Please go across to Solomon's Mercantile and
ask Mr Solomon to see me in my room. You may stand at
the door while he and I converse.'

'*Sí, Patrona,*' Jorge said.

Lilywhite locked the door after Jorge left and opened it
only when she heard his two-tap, one-tap, two-tap code.
The man who stood with Jorge came only to his shoulder,
but there was a power in the craggy lines of his face.
Fredrick Solomon and Lilywhite teamed up nearly a
decade ago, long before Lilywhite met Real Lee.

'Fredrick,' she said.

'Lillian,' he answered.

'Are we ready?'

'We are.'

'And do you agree that this town will see growth and prosper?'

'It will. But it also has a cancer.'

Lilywhite raised her eyebrows in question.

'Benford,' Solomon said. 'He seeks power, but he prefers that others take the risks. He would be a mover amongst us, but lacks the moral strength. Eventually he will fall, but he could cause a good deal of trouble.'

'Will he bother our business?'

'Perhaps, but not at the moment. He likes to take over, not build.'

'Then we open Swan's Lake on schedule.'

'We do,' Solomon said, 'or should I say, you do.'

'Thank you, Fredrick. You've done well, as always.' Lilywhite's smile was radiant. She treasured Solomon's skills and wanted him to know it.

Solomon bowed stiffly to Lilywhite and left the room. Jorge stayed.

Lilywhite stared out the cloudy window. She always moved decisively, but could never shake the clutch of fear in her stomach. This time, would she fail?

'*Patrona*?'

Lilywhite turned to face the big Mexican. 'Yes?'

'As I would cross *el camino, Patrona,* six *hombres* rode by me. They were dusty and dry, so it must have been a long ride. Five rode straight in their saddles. One slumped. Five had fine sombreros, though dusty. . . .'

'What is it, Jorge?'

Jorge looked directly into his patrona's eyes. 'One man wore no sombrero, *Patrona.* His face was battered, bloody, and one eye was swollen closed. I thought maybe he clung to consciousness only by his strong will.'

'Jorge. What was it?'

'Him, *Patrona*. The man was Real Lee.'

Lilywhite's hands flew to cover her mouth. Her eyes widened. 'Real?' she whispered. 'Real Lee?'

Jorge nodded. '*Sí, Patrona*,' he said. 'Beaten and bloody, *Patrona*, but Jorge would recognize Señor Real anywhere. *Sin duda*. It was him.'

'Who were the men?'

Jorge shrugged. 'Gunmen, *supongo que sí*. One wore fine clothes and *mustaches*. He bore cruelty in his eyes.'

'Find them, Jorge,' Lilywhite said.

'*Sí, Padrona*.'

After Jorge left, Lilywhite sat on the edge of the bed. How long had it been since Real Lee left her in Globe City? Three years? Four? She'd not forgotten Real Lee. Had he forgotten her?

'Hello the fire,' Lightning called. 'Me and Sparrow are coming in.'

A gray line started to outline the Mazatal Mountains, the first sign of dawn. The fragrance of fresh coffee had already spread across the campsite. Down on the flat, cabins still smoked, but the fires were out. Wilder had the watch. Finn lay rolled in his blanket. Tom Easter was in his lean-to.

'More horses than two,' Wilder called.

'Company,' Lightning replied. He and Sparrow rode into sight leading four horses with gagged riders tied to their saddles.

'Company, eh?' Wilder strode into camp. 'What for?'

'These rowdies was holding more'n a thousand head of Cibie cattle in that box canyon off Bull Tank. We turned the cows on to the range and brought this company back with us. Figured Tom Easter might want to talk to them.'

86

Lightning's gray eyes sharpened as he took stock of the camp. Finn McBride stamped his feet into his boots and stood up. Tom Easter came from his lean-to. Lightning looked around again. 'Where's Real Lee?' he said.

Tom Easter toed at a stone. 'We got suckered,' he said. 'Someone set fire to the Assembly's cabins. Real took off like the fires was under his tail – never even saddled up. Time we got saddled and down the hill, he was gone. Whoever did it laid for him.'

'What're you doing here?' Lightning's tone was hard and sharp. 'Why ain't you after them bastards?'

'Still dark, Lightning,' Wilder said. 'Not you or me or even Sparrow can track through the night. We'll hit the trail hard when it gets light.'

'I don't like it,' Tom Easter said. 'We all go riding off after Real and there's no one watching over Respite.'

'I'm going,' Lightning said. 'I'm just extra in this crew anyway.' The birds started to twitter as the dawn neared. 'How 'bout you?' he said to Sparrow.

'I go with Lightning?' Sparrow said to Wilder.

'Go,' Wilder said.

'Good.' Lightning waved at the four gagged riders. 'I reckon these cracker-asses ain't regular with Tate's gang. Nobody should be that easy to injun up on. But they may know something. Up to you, Tom Easter.'

Lightning dismounted and led Patches to a stand of chamise. 'You eat now, pard,' he said. 'We'll be riding 'fore long.' He slipped the bridle from the horse's mouth and left it dangling from his neck. He slid his Winchester from the scabbard and dug into his saddle-bags for the cleaning kit he'd bought with the gun.

At the fire, Lightning sat on one of the rocks they'd set around the fire as seats and began cleaning the

Winchester. He jacked all the cartridges into his hat, left the action open, and wiped everything well with a scrap of cotton flour sacking. He screwed the ramrod together and pushed a bit of oiled cloth back and forth through the barrel.

'You'll ride better with a cup of coffee or two in you,' Wilder said. He offered Lightning a tin cup full of dark coffee.

Lightning said nothing, but nodded and took the cup. He sipped at it, grimaced, then set it down and continued cleaning the rifle. He dribbled oil into the action, then worked the lever a half dozen times. The movement was smooth and the only sound was the slick swish of oiled metal against oiled metal. He wiped away the excess oil and then buffed each cartridge with the same cloth before loading the bullets into the Winchester. Then he started on his Remington Army.

'He's a tough man,' Wilder said. 'Real Lee's not going under easy. He'll take a lot of killing.'

Lightning said nothing. He took another sip of coffee and worked on the Remington.

Finn McBride baked biscuits in his little Dutch oven. Bacon sizzled in a frying pan. The four riders sat their horses, bound and gagged. Gradually, the land got lighter. The cabins below gave off wisps of smoke. Lightning finished cleaning his six-gun. He shoved it into its holster, drank the rest of his coffee, then stowed the gun-cleaning kit back in his saddle-bags and shoved the Winchester into its scabbard.

'You'd better have something to eat, boy,' Finn said, holding out a biscuit and bacon sandwich.

'Watch who you call boy,' Lightning said. But he took the food.

Finn grinned. 'You're a man, son. No kidding. No offense meant. But my boy Will is only a couple of years shy of you. How old are you, anyway?'

Lightning took a big bite of the biscuit and bacon. He didn't answer Finn until he'd chewed and swallowed. 'I'll be sixteen come November,' he said.

Finn stood silent for a long moment. 'Well, you ask me, you're a man, Lightning. But there's still a thing or two you'll have to learn along the way.'

'Whatever you say, Mr McBride, I got a job to do. Real Lee's about the only man who's ever treated me straight, one to one. If he's in trouble, it's naturally up to me to do whatever I can to help.' Lightning took another bite and. held the half-eaten sandwich up in salute. 'Good,' he said, his mouth still half-full.

'If my Laurel was here, she'd tell you not to talk with your mouth full,' Finn said. He chuckled.

Lightning showed a ghost of a smile. Then he gobbled the rest of the food, gulped water from the camp canteen, and went to check on his horse. He returned leading Patches by the reins.

Sparrow stood from where he'd squatted by the fire, still chewing. He finished his coffee and put the cup in the dishpan. After he fetched his gray mare, he pointed to a line of hoof prints dug into the dry dirt. 'Wilder says Real Lee spurred his horse there. We follow.'

When they were beyond earshot of the camp, Lightning reined up. Sparrow stopped beside him with a question on his face.

'You didn't have to come, Sparrow,' Lightning said. 'Someone laid for Real Lee. That means they had more than sodbusters on their mind. I figure it'd take more'n a couple of men to take Real Lee down. No telling what we're riding into.'

Sparrow grunted. 'We go,' he said. 'Talk takes time.' His mare seemed to understand, because she started off without Sparrow doing a thing. Sparrow guided her along the trail of hoof prints that showed Sorry at a flat-out run. He waved a hand and Lightning followed.

'Damn,' Lightning swore. *You hang on, Real Lee. Whatever they do to you, wherever you are, we're coming. We'll get you out.*

10

They rode into town in broad daylight. Despite Real Lee bearing the bruises and blood of a thorough beating, Kyle Benford and his gunnies went down Main Street as if they owned it. They paid no attention to the Mexican standing in front of the Stockman Hotel.

'Take him to the house,' Benford said. 'I'll see to him later.'

Benford's men peeled off at the trail called Frontier Street. Broad where it intersected Main Street, the would-be thoroughfare soon turned into a narrow wagon track that wound around a low hill toward the abandoned Fort McDonald.

Benford had built a house on the far side of Sagacity Ridge, a place not easily seen by casual travelers. Benford's men took Real Lee to that house, but they didn't invite him in to the guest room. They took him to a dugout carved into the side of the ridge. They took him there to chain him.

A thick set man with a two-week growth of black beard and a walrus moustache untied Real's legs and released his hands from the saddlehorn, but left them tied together. He gave Real's left arm a strong jerk. Real tumbled from

91

the saddle and hit the ground hard on his left shoulder. One more stab of pain joined those from his battered face and ribs.

'Up, asshole,' the man said. 'You think you got troubles now, well, it's been a church sociable so far.'

Real struggled to his feet and stood there, head hanging. His breath rasped in his ravaged throat. After a moment, he managed to lift his head. 'Don't recognize you, cowboy. Give me a name so's I'll know you when we meet on even terms,' he said.

The thick set man backhanded Real with a huge closed fist. Real saw it coming and collapsed, lessening the force of the blow.

'The name's Bouchard, asshole, but most people call me Butcher.' He kicked Real for emphasis. 'Bring him,' he said to the others.

Two men dragged Real into the root cellar, where Butcher held the slanting door open.

'Stand him up over there,' Butcher said.

The men hefted Real to his feet and stood him against the wall. Butcher lifted one arm and then the other, fitting them into iron shackles that hung from the low ceiling by short chains.

Butcher stepped back and stood looking at Real in disdain. 'I hear you're tough shit, Real Lee. Well, we'll see just how tough you are, later.'

Butcher and the men left. Real stood against a dirt wall in the dark, his arms held out at shoulder length by the shackles.

He stood, and he stood, and he stood. The shackles weren't too tight, but not loose enough that he could pull his hands through them. When his eyes got used to the dark, he found that cracks in the planks of the door let some light into his prison, but not enough to see anything of his surroundings. His bruises throbbed. The cuts inside his mouth no longer bled. He tongued the gap were a tooth had been. Breathing hurt, but not with the sharp stabs of pain brought by broken ribs. Thank God for small favors.

Real tried suspending himself by his arms. The shackles bit into the flesh around the bones of his hands. He stood back up. He finally found a position with his legs spread slightly, his knees locked, his back and head against the wall, and his arms hanging limp in the shackles. The chains supported the weight of his arms, and he could stand the bite of the shackles on his hands. Real closed his eyes. If Sorry could sleep standing up, so could he. Couldn't he?

Real actually dozed. Somehow his knees stayed locked. Maybe he didn't actually sleep, but he nodded off. All the aches came together into a dull pounding that throbbed in time with his heartbeat. The light filtering through the cracks in the door planks turned blue, then gray, then went as dark as the inside of the cellar. A cricket chirped, but Real didn't notice. He stood, and stood, and stood.

The muscles in his legs got hard as iron. They cramped, but he couldn't rub them. He yelled at them. No one heard, least of all the cramping muscles.

Real worked his legs a little farther apart, changing the stress on his muscles. The cramps went away, but more of his weight fell on his wrists. His arm muscles stretched. The shackles bit. Dozing was a thing of the past.

'Damn you, Real Lee,' he grumbled aloud. 'You shoulda stayed in Africa. People were gentler there. They'd just cut off your arm. Or your head. An' if they cut off your head, nothing mattered anyway. Gentler in Africa.

Not butchers, them Muslims. Gentle.'

In his well of pain, time lost meaning. Real's bladder swelled to bursting. He could do nothing but allow the warm fluid to fill his crotch and run down his legs. If he hadn't hurt so much, he might have been ashamed. As it was, he hardly noticed. He hardly noticed the tears trickling down his face. And he hardly noticed the heavy door swing open.

'God it stinks in here.' A hand slapped Real's face. 'Rat! Shit-faced Rat. You'll strain to attention when your Dyke speaks to you, Rat. ATTENTION!'

In his mind, Real went back to Lexington and VMI. He struggled to strain, to reach the exaggerated position of attention that VMI upperclassmen demanded of the school's Rat Mass, but the shackles kept his arms spread wide. The best he could do was brace himself straight up against the wall.

'What a godawful stench, Rat.' A face shoved itself into Real's line of sight. A face full of hate and scorn. A face from his days at VMI.

'Dyke Seffleck, Sir,' he managed to mumble. 'Dyke, sir, yes, sir.'

Benford laughed. 'I promised you, Rat Lee. I promised you on the parade ground that I'd get you like I'd get that shithead Cadell. Anyone could see CSA had no chance to win the war. And asshole Breckinridge ordered the Cadet Corps to fight on the losing side. No way.'

The dark cellar went silent. Benford watched Real, who strived to stand absolutely still, at attention against the wall, his arms spread wide by the iron shackles. All he needed was a cross.

'I see you're on your way to learning the obedience a Rat should have,' Benford said. 'You've pissed your pants,

Rat. That means you've been drinking too much water.'
He stepped close to Real and shouted, spraying spittle.
'No water. No food. No rest. Rat, there's only one thing
lower than a Rat. Whale shit. And whale shit's all at the
bottom of the ocean. Think about that, Rat.'

Benford stormed out of the cellar, slamming the thick
door closed with a thud.

'Muslims,' Real mumbled. 'Give me Muslims any day.'
He let his leg muscles relax. All he could do was stand.

Lightning and Sparrow rode into Payson late in the afternoon. They'd found where Real Lee was dragged from his
horse. They'd found his broken tooth where he got beat
up. And they found a trail of hoof prints that led straight
to Payson.

They rode up Beeline and turned on to Main. By habit,
Lightning loosened his Remington in its holster.
Businesses lined the street with Solomon's Mercantile on
the corner, doors opening on both Beeline and Main.
Close to Solomon's, a smaller building housed an assay
office and a millinery. Main Street was wide enough for a
four-horse team and wagon to turn around. A dog lay in
the dust under the porch at Solomon's, tongue lolling.

Halfway down the block, the Stockman Hotel took
center stage. As Lightning and Sparrow rode by, a large
Mexican with a silver-plated pistol in a black gun rig deco-
rated by silver conchos leaned nonchalantly against the
wall to the left of the door. He watched as they passed.
Sparrow nodded, one Mexican to another, and the man
nodded back, a slight smile on his broad face.

'Man to steer clear of,' Lightning said.

'Half-breed,' Sparrow said.

'All the more reason.'

The parade of saloons began.

The Branding Iron dominated the north side of the street, with the Ox Bow opposite, the Monarch down the way, and a rundown affair with a faded sign that read 'PRIME WHISKEY 10¢' at the end.

'I'm going to raise a ruckus,' Lightning said. 'Starting with the biggest place in town.'

Sparrow nodded. 'No one notices a sparrow,' he said. 'I will be near.'

Lightning reined Patches in at the hitching rail in front of the Branding Iron. He pulled the Remington from its holster, added a sixth bullet to the cylinder and gave it a spin, then replaced the six-gun. He dismounted and tethered Patches to the rail before mounting the steps to the porch that ran the length of the saloon front. The late afternoon sun painted everything with gold, and in spite of the early hour, the tinkle of a piano came from inside, accompanied by the rumble of voices and punctuated by shrill female laughter. Lightning shoved his way through the batwing doors.

A few men looked up as he came in, then turned back to whatever they were doing when they saw a young boy in faded maroon shirt and old trousers. He stood for a moment, setting the layout of the room in his mind. Maybe a dozen men, not counting the piano player, and three doves. No shotgun guard in the high chair. Good. Broad-shouldered man behind the bar. Probably Irish. Likely had a shotgun under the counter.

'Whacha want, kid?' the barkeep said when Lightning put his elbows on the bar.

'Got any sarsaparilla?'

'Shit. Ain't growed up enough to have a man's drink, eh?'

Lightning's grin did not reach his eyes. 'Not for you to decide, old man,' he said. 'Just give me the drink.' He plonked a dime on the bar.

Mumbling to himself, the 'keep went to the other end of the long bar and fumbled among some bottles beneath the counter. Lightning stepped to the open end of the bar and lifted a sawed-off Savage shotgun from its pegs.

'Hey!' the barkeep shouted.

Lightning checked the scattergun's loads, snapped it shut, and eared back the hammers. 'I'm looking for Real Lee,' he said, his voice loud enough for everyone in the bar to hear. 'I been hunting Real Lee. Looked for him in Globe City. Sunset, too. But he keeps ahead of me. I heard he might be in Payson, so here I am. Time for Real Lee and me to see which man is best. Now. Where is he?'

Lightning held the cocked Savage in his left hand. His right hand hung near the butt of his Remington.

'Boy?' A man in a white shirt and black leather vest raised his hands shoulder high, palms out. 'I'm going to stand up, boy. Don't you shoot me.'

Lightning said nothing.

The man slowly stood.

'So. You're standing. Where's Real Lee?'

'Do you see him in here?'

'You Real Lee?'

The man barked a short laugh. 'If I were, you'd be dead.'

'You think you can take me, old man?'

'No. I won't even try. But Tag Eidelbaur's in town, and he eats kids like you for breakfast. Take my advice. Clear out.'

'What's your name, that I should listen to you?' Lightning lifted his upper lip in a sneer.

'Frank Decker. But most people just call me Shark.'

'OK, Shark.' Lightning let the hammers of the Savage down and put it back behind the bar. 'I'll look for Real Lee at the Ox Bow. And if he ain't there, I'll go to the Monarch. If I don't find him in Payson, I'll go to Flagstaff. The day will come, I swear, when Real Lee an' me will face off and have it out.' Lightning took two steps toward the batwings, then turned back toward Shark.

'You'd better keep moving, kid,' Shark said.

'Shark, eh? I reckon you figure the cards are in your favor. Maybe you and I can have it out with the pasteboards one day.'

'At your service. . . .'

'Lightning. Just call me Lightning.' With his hand on the butt of his Remington, Lightning pushed through the batwings and walked across the dusty street to the Ox Bow. He left the full glass of sarsaparilla on the bar, untouched.

Real Lee wasn't in the Ox Bow either, but when Lightning came out, a slight man in a bowler hat and tweeds stood in the street. His cheek ticked.

Lightning paid him no attention, angling across Main toward the Monarch.

'You want Real Lee,' the man said, 'you gotta go through me.'

Lightning stopped.

Now both men stood in the middle of Main.

Lightning turned to face the man. 'You know where Real Lee is?'

The man knocked the tail of his coat back behind the butt of his Colt. 'No,' he said.

'I got nothing to do with you, then.'

'No gunman walks away from Tag Edelbauer,' he said. His feet were shoulder-width apart and his right hand

98

hung naturally near the handle of the Colt.

'Never heard of no one called Tag Edelbauer,' Lightning said, and suddenly his Remington was in his hand.

Edelbauer's gun hand didn't even have time to twitch. His face took on the pallor of a man looking death in the face. His hands gradually rose, palms out. 'Take it easy, kid. Just take it easy.'

'What was you saying about Real Lee? Where is he?'

'I don't know and I don't care.'

'Then why are you bracing me?'

'Can't let some kid barge in on my range. Shit.'

People began to gather, to watch what was going on between a youngster with a big Remington in his hand and the man with a gunman's reputation in Payson.

'Walk away, Edelbauer,' Lightning said. 'I may be young, but I'm no killer. And I figure you don't want to die. Let me tell you this. If I see you coming at me again, you will die. I swear I'll kill you. And don't think I can't.' He holstered the Remington and walked toward the Monarch, even though he knew Real Lee would not be there.

Edelbauer watched Lightning enter the bar, then made his own way to the Branding Iron.

When Lightning emerged from the Monarch, a big broad-faced Mexican waited for him. 'A moment, *señor*,' the Mexican said. 'I am Jorge Valenzuela. *Mi Patrona* wishes a word with you, *por favor*.'

Lightning hesitated. He flashed a look around, but didn't see Sparrow.

'Your friend is close by,' Jorge said. 'His people and mine are old enemies, Yaqui and Apache, but those times have passed.'

Lightning nodded. 'I'll go. Lead on.'

Jorge made a tiny bow, turned on his heel, and strode toward the Stockman Hotel. He didn't look back to see if Lightning followed.

Sparrow appeared as Lightning and Jorge neared the hotel. The sun dipped below the western mountains, and a man in shirtsleeves and oiled hair climbed a ladder to light the lantern that hung from a pole outside the Stockman lobby. A well-weathered wagon, filled with supplies from Solomon's, clattered west on Main, passing the three men. The driver on the wagon's seat, a miner by his dress, ignored them.

They entered the lobby, climbed the stairs to the second floor, and walked down the lamp-lit hall. Jorge stopped at the door of the corner room overlooking Main and Beeline. He knocked – one knock, two, one, and two again. The door opened and Lightning stood stock still, his mouth open. He'd never seen such a beautiful woman.

'Come in,' the angel said. 'My name is Lillian Whitehead, but my friends call me Lilywhite.'

11

'Jorge tells me you are rightly called Lightning and you are seeking a man named Real Lee,' Lilywhite said.

Lightning came to, shook his head, tipped his hat, and said, 'Yes, ma'am. Real Lee is my friend. Someone laid for him over in Green Valley, and me and Sparrow here tracked them to Payson.'

'Hmmm.'

'I tried to raise some ruckus in the saloons, ma'am, but no one bit. A gunman that called himself Tag Edelbauer tried to brace me though. We didn't talk much.'

'Real Lee came to Payson,' Lilywhite said. 'Jorge saw him.'

'You know Real Lee?' Lightning said to Jorge.

'*Sí.*'

Sparrow spoke. 'Lightning. Sorry's trail leads away. I found his footprints.'

'Where?'

'I heard someone say the way is called Frontier.'

Lightning tipped his hat to Lilywhite again. 'If it's just the same with you, ma'am, me and Sparrow will be following Sorry's trail.'

'Sorry?'

'Yes, ma'am. That's what Real Lee calls his sorrel horse. Sorry's offside fore hoof splays to the right somewhat.'

'Come on, Sparrow, we got a horse to follow.'

'*Señor. Momentito. Patrona, con su permisso,* I would ride with these *hombres.* I will return with Señor Real Lee.' Jorge said.

'Excuse me, ma'am,' Lightning said. He strode from the room, lightfooted it down the stairs, and burst from the hotel door. A group of horsemen rode by, headed toward Beeline. Lightning glanced at them, then looked again. Tag Edelbaur rode a step behind the dandy-looking man in the lead. *Now where's a gunman like Edelbaur headed,* he thought. 'Where's the trail, Sparrow?' he asked.

Sparrow led the way back to their horses, which were still hitched to the rail in front of the Branding Iron. They mounted, and Sparrow turned his gray mare's head toward Frontier Street. Jorge joined them, mounted on a big bay stallion. The bay pranced, and Jorge touched the butt of the Winchester thrust into a saddle scabbard beneath his right leg.

'*Hombres,*' he said. '*Vamanos.*'

Sorry's distinctive hoofprints led up Frontier Street, past the new three-story building that would house Lilywhite's Swan's Lake, and away from Payson. The three men rode north toward a low ridge. On the right, a man and a boy worked on a new house, nailing twelve-inch planks to two-by-four framing with ten-penny nails.

Lightning pulled his Remington and checked its loads. Six .44 caliber shells. He spun the cylinder and tested the action, then put the six-gun back in its holster. He felt the bullets in his gunbelt. There were twenty-three. His .44-.40 Winchester had fourteen in its magazine. If they got into a shooting fight, he had forty three bullets. That would

102

have to be enough.

Sorry's hoofprints led them out and around a low ridge, then left on to the main wagon track. Sparrow waved the other riders to a halt. 'I go see,' he said. 'Stay here.'

Lightning said, '*Cuidao*,' and reined Patches toward an open space sheltered by a stand of Ponderosa, and sat cross-legged on the carpet of pine needles. A red-headed woodpecker tapped away at one of the Ponderosas and a blue jay bobbed among the branches of an alligator juniper.

Jorge sat his bay for some moments before joining Lightning. The two men said nothing, but their silence lay comfortably on their shoulders.

'Miss Lilywhite's sure pretty,' Lightning said at last.

'*La Patrona* loves Real Lee,' Jorge said.

'Oh.'

Silence again. This time not so comfortable.

'Real never said nothing,' Lightning said.

Jorge shrugged. 'Señor Lee says nothing about himself.'

'Yeah.'

Sparrow appeared, moving through the brush without a sound. He carried his Winchester and his big Bowie seemed more prominent. He wore a dirty cloth headband instead of his usual sombrero. He looked Apache.

'One big house,' Sparrow said. 'Big barn, too. I see two men. Maybe more inside. Sorry horse in corral with two more. Two tied in front of house.' It was a long speech for Sparrow.

Lightning looked at Jorge. 'Me and Jorge will ride up to the house,' he said. 'That OK with you, Jorge?'

'*Si.*'

'You do what you usually do, Sparrow. OK?'

Sparrow nodded and slipped off into the woods. The woodpecker stopped tapping.

Lightning and Jorge mounted up. 'Let's go,' Lightning said. He pulled the Remington from its holster to check it once more.

The approach to the house was cleared and offered no cover for at least two hundred yards. Behind it, the sharp rise of the ridge made attack from that direction untenable. A barn stood off to the right and somewhat behind the house. Not the roomy barn of a working spread, but one that might be found on a country estate, its sides painted brick red with white accents.

'Man in the loft,' Jorge said, his voice just loud enough for Lightning to hear.

'See him.'

The front door of the house opened and a giant of a man emerged. The Winchester in his hand looked like a toothpick. Two more men followed him, spreading out, one to his left and one to his right.

Lightning rode straight ahead, hands on the saddle horn. 'You take the *hombre* on the right,' he said to Jorge. 'Wait for my move, *por favor.*' He felt a little strange, a youngster of fifteen giving orders to a fighting man like Jorge, but Jorge had come along on Lightning's job, so it was up to Lightning to get it done.

The giant jacked a shell into the chamber of his Winchester as Lightning and Jorge closed on the house.

Lightning reined Patches to a stop. Jorge on his big bay stallion halted slightly behind Lightning and four or five steps off to the right. The man in the hayloft was no longer visible. Lightning didn't worry about it. His attention focused on the huge man on the front porch.

' 'Day to you,' Lightning said.

104

'What in hell do you want?'

'You don't sound neighborly,' Lightning said.

'Then get the hell out of here.'

'Yeah. Maybe. But I got a question for you.'

The big man stood stolid and silent. Then, 'What?'

'I'm looking for Real Lee,' Lightning said. 'Tell me where he is, and you won't have to die.'

'Die? You're shitting me. A shavetail kid and a Mex? Two of you. Three of us, with guns cocked and ready? You wanna try?'

'Where's Real Lee?'

The big man's eyes flickered.

'Reckon you're not telling me all you know, old man. I'll ask you one more time. You don't answer with what you know, and I'll have a look around on my own.'

'Like hell you will.'

'Oh, I will. It ain't up to you. Where. Is. Real. Lee?'

The big man made the mistake of trying to raise the Winchester to his shoulder.

'Now!' Lightning shouted. He lunged from Patches' saddle, his Remington already in hand. He fired as he fell, and the slug took the big man in the joint of his right shoulder, shattering bone and tearing cartilage. The Winchester clattered down the front steps and went off as it hit the ground.

A split second after Lightning's shot, Jorge's nickel-plated Colt roared once, twice, and the rifleman on the right crumpled. The third man dropped his rifle as if it were red hot, and raised his hands. 'Don't shoot. Don't shoot.'

Lightning cushioned his fall with an elbow and a shoulder. He rolled and came up with his Remington Army pointed at the big man. 'Where's Real Lee?' He thumbed the hammer back.

'I need a doc,' the big man whimpered.

Sparrow pushed a fourth man around the corner of the house. He bled slightly from a shallow slice across his throat. 'No more men,' Sparrow said.

The big man groaned, trying to stem the flow of blood from his shattered shoulder. He slumped against the wall. Lightning climbed the steps and grabbed a handful of the giant's hair. 'I asked you a question, lump of shit. Where. Is. Real. Lee?'

Another groan. The man's eyes rolled back in his head. He collapsed to the floor.

'Shit.'

'Kid?' the third man said in a tentative voice. 'Kid?'

'You got something to say, rat's ass?' Lightning's frustration marked every word.

'Kid, I don't know if it's the man called Real Lee that you're looking for, but the boss's got a man hanging in the root cellar out back.'

'Watch 'em,' Lightning said to Jorge.

'*Sí.*'

Lightning pounded down the steps and plunged around the corner, eyes raking the grounds for sign of a root cellar. He saw a door set into the slant of the ridge. It had to be it. He ran.

A crossbar held the door closed against anyone trying to open it from the inside, though Lightning didn't register that fact as he tore it from its brackets and tossed it aside. He pulled the heavy door open and let it fall back against the slope.

Lightning drew his Remington, thumbing the hammer back as the gun left the holster. He moved quickly into the dark maw of the dugout, stepping sharply to the left as he entered. He leaned against the dirt wall and waited for his eyes to adjust. Slowly he could make out the inside of the cellar. Iron tongs. A long stave. Oversized pliers. Branding irons. Stuff that Lightning couldn't put a name to. And at the back of the cellar, a man. Arms cuffed and strung from the ceiling by chains. Legs spread. Back against the wall. Head hanging.

'Real!'

The man didn't move.

'Real!' Lightning intended to shout, but it came from his mouth as a scream.

Then Sparrow was there. He touched his friend's shoulder. 'Come,' he said.

Lightning followed, gathering his self-control.

Together, Lightning and Sparrow unshackled the manacles from Real Lee's wrists and carried him to the house.

Water and some bread from the kitchen helped Real revive. Bread and water never tasted so good. Sips at first, then deep swallows, and finally he chugalugged a whole quart.

'Found this, Real,' Lightning said. He held a can of peaches. 'Can you eat some?'

Real tried to grin. 'I'm getting there, Lightning. Back amongst the living. Damn. I figured Seffleck had me pegged out and drawn for sure.'

Lightning cut the top off the can with his Barlow knife. 'Best sharpen m'knife after that,' he said. He gave the can to Real and handed him a good-sized spoon. 'This here house's got pert-near anything a man could want.'

Real Lee stood up on shaky legs, can in hand. He drank the sweet syrup straight from the container, then shovelled fruit into his mouth with the spoon. The can was empty in

107

two heartbeats more than a minute.

'I'm going to the outhouse,' Real said. 'See if you can scare me up a pair of britches.' He went out the back door under his own power, stretching a hand out now and again to steady himself on a wall or a chair back or a door frame. When he returned, Lightning held a pair of striped California pants and Real's gun rig.

'A man never knows what he's missing until he's not shit for three days,' Real said. He stripped, union suit and all.

'Jesus,' Lightning said. 'I ain't never seen a man with so many scars. Shit.'

Real pulled on the pants, added his shirt, then buckled the rig around his hips. 'There. I'm dressed again, or would be, if I had my hat.' He ignored Lightning's comment about the scars.

'Couldn't find your hat,' Lightning said, 'but I got your tooth.'

Real chuckled. He hugged himself. 'Can't seem to get warm,' he said. 'Wonder if there's a coat of some kind in this place that a man could borrow?'

'I'll look,' Lightning said.

Real's legs trembled. He scrubbed a shaking hand across his stubbled face. God. And he'd thought himself a tough, hard man. *When will Seffleck be back?* He had to get away. Another round of Dyke Seffleck's hazing might be more than he could take. Get away!

'Take your pick, Real.' Lightning held a sheepskin jacket in one hand and a dark gray frock-coat in the other.

Real tried both and chose the frock. It came down halfway to his knees and kept more of him warm.

'Gotta get out of here,' he said to no one in particular. 'Gotta leave.'

108

'Sorry's saddled and ready, Real. Ready to go whenever you are.'

'Let's do it.' Real took shaky steps toward the front door.

'Some gunnies on the porch,' Lightning said. 'Wanna talk to them?'

With his hand on the doorknob, Real said, 'I do.'

Four men lay on the porch – one dead, one wounded, and two trussed like hogs for market. The wounded one had called himself Butcher when he slapped Real Lee and punched him around in the cellar.

'Butcher,' Real said.

The big man groaned.

Real toed his shattered shoulder.

Butcher screamed and his eyes flew open. 'Jay-sus!'

'Hello, Butcher. Tell me something.'

'Doctor. Shit. Help.'

Real put a hand on the porch rail and squatted next to the man who'd tormented him. 'Nearest doc is in Globe City, unless you want to try the Army sawbones at Camp Verde.' He took a deep breath. 'The shoulder's not bleeding much but the bullet's still in there. I'd say you'll live at least until Seffleck gets here.'

'S-s-seffleck?'

'Yeah. Ben Seffleck. This is his house, I reckon.'

'House? Benford's house?' Butcher moaned. 'House's Kyle Benford's.'

Real stood up. 'Shit. Who in Hell is Kyle Benford?' Again Real's question was directed at no one in particular, but he vaguely remembered the man who'd said he was Real's worst nightmare. He's called himself Kyle Benford.

'*Señor?*' Jorge held the reins to Real's sorrel horse. '*El caballo*, she is ready.'

Real's face lit with a slow grin. 'Jorge. *Hombre mas malo.* Lilywhite here?'

'*Sí, señor.*'

'Where?'

'Stockman Hotel, *señor.*'

Real turned his head towards Lightning. 'Mind if we take the long way back to Green Valley? I'd like to see Lilywhite.'

'Can do. But what about them?' He waved at the men on the porch.

'Someone'll come along. Let's ride.' Real reached for Sorry's reins, stepped down from the porch, and made as if to mount, but couldn't lift his foot to stirrup height. Lightning started, as if to help, but Jorge stopped him with an upheld hand.

Real looked around. The stump of an old oak sat halfway to the barn, its roots still solid in the ground. Real led Sorry to the stump, climbed up on it, stuck a foot in the stirrup, and mounted his horse. 'Man's gotta ride his own broncs,' he muttered, and reined Sorry toward the others.

'You'll be wanting this,' Lightning said. He held a Winchester rifle up where Real could grasp it. 'Ain't mine, but who the Hell cares?' Real said. He checked the rifle's loads and shoved it into the saddle scabbard beneath the offside stirrup leather. When he handled guns, his hands didn't shake. He took a deep breath. 'Them jehus wanted me outta Green Valley for some reason. I've got a bad feeling that Pearson Tate may be taking his gunnies, Tag Eidelbauer and Amos Dwyer and them, over to Respite to hit the Assembly.'

'Tag Eidelbauer?' Lightning said.

'Yeah. He's one of them hired to run out the Assembly, remember?'

110

'Shit.'

'Watch your mouth, kid,' Real said, a grin on his face.

'Real. Tag Eidelbauer and a bunch of riders was leaving town when we started out here looking for you.'

Real reined Sorry toward the wagon trail. 'Come on, then. No time to waste.' He gigged Sorry into a gallop.

12

'Real!' Lilywhite put a hand to her mouth. Her eyes took in Real's battered face, his stiff step, and baggy pants and too-long frock coat that obviously were not his own.

'Lily.' Real automatically reached to tip his hat, forgetting for a moment that he was bareheaded. 'It's mighty good to see you,' he said.

Lilywhite reached for his hands. 'It's been too long, Real. Much too long.'

Real nodded, then said, 'You'd best not get too close, Lily. I'm not all that fragrant.'

She hugged him anyway.

'Lily, I need a union suit, some pants that fit, a decent hat, and two boxes of .44-.40 cartridges. Fast.'

'Fred Solomon has a store full.'

'I've got a problem.' Real stared at the floor, then at Lilywhite. As a man, he hated what he had to say. 'Lily, I've got no money. I've been doing some gun work over in Little Green Valley, but haven't been paid yet. And the strongarms Ben Seffleck hired to bushwhack me took all I had.'

Lilywhite turned to Jorge. 'If you please,' she said, 'could you ask Mr Solomon to come to my room? Tell him what Real needs, he knows the sizes. Ask him to hurry, please.'

'*Sí, Patrona.*' The Mexican gunman left.

Sparrow kept to the street, waiting and watching. Lightning stayed close to Real, as if by keeping him in sight, he could protect the battered gunman.

'Lily, they put me in a root cellar, at least it was built like a root cellar, and Ben Seffleck, who was my Dyke at VMI. . . .'

Lilywhite raised her eyebrows. 'Real, darling, I have no idea what a Dyke is.'

'When you enter Virginia Military Institute, even before you're a cadet, you enter as a Rat – the lowest animal God ever made. Your Dyke is a fourth-year cadet that's assigned to torment you. If you can make it through two weeks of pure Hell, you become a VMI Cadet. Ben Seffleck was the Dyke in charge of me.

'Anyway, Seffleck really hated me for some reason. And during the battle at New Market, he killed the Cadet Sergeant, shot him in the back. Then he disappeared.

'He found me somehow and had me shackled in that cellar.' Real's eyebrows knitted. 'Strange, though, when Lightning here busted me out, the gunnies guarding the place said it belonged to Kyle Benford, and I think he was there somewhere.'

'Kyle Benford?'

'That's what the one called Butcher said.'

Lilywhite took a step back. 'Kyle Benford nearly owns this town. The man many call the Butcher is a bouncer at the Branding Iron, Benford's saloon.'

'Makes a man wonder what the connection is between him and Ben Seffleck, doesn't it?'

'I'm sure you'll find out,' Lilywhite said. She hugged

Real again. 'You are entirely correct, darling. Your fragrance is not that of an expensive cologne. There's a pitcher of water and a washcloth next to the commode. Take a moment to wash yourself. You'll feel much better.'

Real began removing his clothes. Lilywhite turned her attention to Lightning. 'Young man, right now Real needs good red meat. Trot down to Ma Becker's, second building up Main Street from the hotel. Tell Maggie I want two thick slices of the roast she's always got in the oven. Tell her it'd better weigh at least a pound when it gets here. Tell her to pile on the mashed potatoes and plenty of her skillet gravy. And bring a loaf of her sourdough, too. Quickly, now. Jorge will be back soon, and Real's in a hurry.'

All Lightning could say in the face of Lilywhite's beauty was 'Yes'm.' He fled.

'Give me that washcloth,' Lilywhite said to Real. 'I'll make sure you're clean.'

'I don't have time to dally, Lily.' Real dipped the washcloth in the basin, wrung out the excess water, and proceeded with his spit bath.

Lilywhite stepped close. 'I never cease to be amazed at the marks life has left on your body,' she said. Her fingers traced the criss-cross scars of the whipping a Muslem caliph gave him in Morocco.

'Lily,' he said. 'I'm not covered. You keep touching me and Lightning will be almighty surprised when he gets back with the roast beef.'

'Give me the washcloth.'

Real handed it to her, indecision on his face.

Lilywhite washed him quickly and thoroughly, without arousing any undue reactions.

When Lightning returned, Real sat on the bed, a towel

114

across his lap. Lilywhite raised the window and tossed the water from the basin into the street below.

'Here you go, Real.'

'Cut the meat up for me, would you, son?'

Lightning sliced the roast into bite-sized pieces with his Barlow knife. His eyes followed the steaming beef as he passed the plate to Real.

'Oh, how thoughtless of me,' Lilywhite said. 'Go back and tell Maggie to make you a big roast beef sandwich.'

'No, ma'am,' Lightning said, 'meaning no disrespect, ma'am.'

Lilywhite put her hands on her hips and raised her eyebrows at Lightning.'

He ducked his head. 'My friend Sparrow's outside, ma'am, keeping watch. I couldn't eat without him getting a fair share.'

Lilywhite laughed. 'Of course. Be sure Maggie makes two sandwiches, one larger than the other, then give the bigger one to Sparrow. And give him my thanks for watching over my Real.'

'Yes'm.' Lightning rushed from the room, roast beef in his eyes.

'Your Lightning seems to be a good boy,' Lilywhite said.

'When's Jorge gonna get here with my clothes? I don't feel right all naked like this.' Real wolfed the roast beef and potatoes, then sopped up the gravy with chunks of sourdough bread.

Lilywhite gave him a wide-eyed smile. 'Darling, you look fine. And I'm sure I'm not the only woman who has appreciated the sight. You eat well, too.'

Real had no answer. He rearranged the towel to hide as much as possible, and slid the empty plate on to the low table at the head of the bed.

115

'Real Lee, I do believe you're blushing.' Lilywhite's laugh sounded like tinkling bells.

A rap came at the door. Then two. And another.

'Come in, Jorge,' Lilywhite called.

Jorge entered with a pile of shirts and trousers, union suit and socks on one arm and two Stetsons in the other hand. '*El comerciante* Señor Solomon sent these. He said you are to choose.' He put the clothing on the bed beside Real and laid the hats on top. He dug two boxes of .44-40 bullets from his pockets and put them on the table beside the empty plate.

'Lightning's gone to Ma Becker's for sandwiches,' Lilywhite said to Jorge. 'Perhaps you'd like something yourself. Just tell Maggie what you want.'

'*Gracias, Patrona.* Señora Maggie always has *chilli con carne y frijoles* on the stove. I like it very much. *Muy delicioso.*'

As soon as Jorge left, Real went through the clothing. He chose a pair of dark gray wool trousers and a lighter gray shirt. Solomon sent only one union suit, tan. 'If you'll turn your back to me, Lily, I'll get dressed,' he said.

'Not a chance,' she said. She stood with her arms folded beneath her breasts and watched Real's every move, her eyes dancing.

He stomped his feet, in new stockings, into his boots, set a black straight-brimmed Stetson on his head, and buckled his gun rig around his hips. Real drew a deep breath.

'Lily, some good people aim to settle at the head of Green Valley, and they're building a dam that'll mean water for everyone, rancher and farmer alike. Well, someone's trying to drive them out. Tom Easter hired me to help those God-fearing folks out, and it looks like Pearson Tate is headed their way with a bunch of guns. I've

116

got to ride to help those people, Lily, but I'll be back. You can count on it.'

'I'll be here.' Lilywhite stood up on tip toes to kiss Real lightly on his split lips. 'I'll be here,' she said again.

'Jorge,' Real said. 'I'm trusting you to watch over Lilywhite while I'm gone.'

'*Positivamente*,' Jorge said, his face flat-planed and hard. 'I am always here.'

'I know. And I thank you. *Gracias, amigo*.'

Real picked up the frock coat from the bed. 'I'll take this along,' he said. He paused when he got to the door. 'I don't know what's happening in Little Green Valley at this moment, Lily, but I owe it to Tom Easter to ride.'

'*Vaya con Dios*,' Jorge said.

'Yes. *Vaya con Dios*, darling.' Lilywhite turned away.

Real Lee clattered down the stairs, strode through the lobby of the Stockman Hotel, and out on to the boardwalk in front. Lightning and Sparrow leaned against the hitching rail, wolfing monstrous roast beef sandwiches.

'Let's ride,' Real said.

Lightning and Sparrow stuffed the remainder of the sandwiches into their mouths and mounted their horses. Real Lee and his two saddle partners left Payson, riding south on Beeline at an easy lope. They could only hope they'd reach Respite in time.

Four miles south on Beeline, Real motioned Sparrow into the lead. 'Take us through Round Valley,' he said. 'Quicker we get to Respite, the better.'

Sparrow picked a trail as only a Jicarilla can. The moonless night made no difference. At times the horses had to walk, but mostly they moved ahead at a brisk trot, and occasionally they could gallop.

Wolf Wilder met them a mile shy of the camp on the

117

hogback overlooking Respite. 'Heard you coming a way off,' he said. 'Sometimes it pays to ride quiet like. Specially in the dark.'

'Save it,' Real barked. Then he backed off. 'You're right, Wolf.'

Wilder grunted.

'No shooting in these parts?'

'None. Why?'

'Pearson Tate had a half-day start on us out of Payson. I figured he was headed for Respite.'

'Ain't seen him. Only movement was Walt Lambert and his dam builders coming in last night. They always come back to Respite for Sunday meetings.'

'Shit. That's where Tate went. He wanted to get the men first.' Real reined Sorry around Wilder. 'They'll be coming,' he said, 'and we'd better be ready. How many riders did you see, Lightning?'

'I never counted,' Lightning said, 'but more'n a dozen, I'd say.'

Wilder trotted toward camp, easily keeping pace with the three men on horseback.

Tom Easter and Finn McBride stood with rifles ready when Real and the others rode in. They lowered the guns when they saw who it was.

'Jaysus,' Finn said. 'What happened to your face?'

'Wasn't watching where I was going,' Real said. 'Ran into a fist or two, but that's not what we're facing. Pearson Tate and a tribe of gunnies'll be riding in any minute.'

'Saddle up,' Tom Easter said. He picked up his saddle and strode for the picket line, followed by Finn and Wilder.

In the gray of dawn, Real stood at the top of the hogback, looking down at Respite. Whoever laid it out

118

hadn't worried about defense. With the Apache tribes mostly on reservations, Jackson probably didn't worry about raids or attacks, or maybe it was just his trust in God.

'I don't reckon they'll try anything military like,' he said, mostly to himself. He naturally saw the lay of the land as a battleground. And he knew that soldiers on the ground had the advantage over fighters on horses. Accurate shooting from horseback was a contradiction in terms. Couldn't be done . . . usually.

'Lightning, you skedaddle over there and hunker down behind that old log. See it?'

'I see it, Real. Where you gonna be?'

'In Respite.'

'I'd rather be with you.'

Real peered at Lightning. 'I appreciate that, son, but I need someone on the flank. Someone I know won't panic. That's you.'

Lightning nodded. 'Count on me,' he said.

Real turned to Sparrow. 'You're free,' he said. 'Don't let them see you. Take the horses down if you can, though I'd rather not hurt horses, but we need men. Not mounts.'

Sparrow nodded, led his gray mare to the picket line, then disappeared into the junipers.

Real raised his voice. 'Fal Wilder.'

'Yeah.'

'You still carry that one-in-a-thousand '73?'

'Yeah.'

'Could you find a place where you can do some long-range shooting?'

'Yeah.'

'Good. Don't have to tell you to pick 'em careful, eh?'

'Nope.' Wilder reined his horse away toward high ground and a grove of cottonwoods south of Respite along

Little Green Valley Creek.

Tom Easter and Finn McBride sat their horses in silence. When it came to tactics, they looked to Real Lee, veteran of the battle at New Market and skirmishes with the Berbers in Morocco.

'Tom, Finn, y'all ride to Respite with me. Pearson Tate's only seen me and only heard Finn. He'll not be expecting a lot of gunfire from Respite. We'll get down among the cabins and find a good place to shoot from. Say Finn, how much dynamite do you have?'

'Dam builders damn near cleaned me out,' McBride said. 'Only got a couple or three sticks left.'

'Save 'em for when we really need 'em,' Real said. 'Now, let's go.'

Three of four horsemen rode down the hogback toward the waking village, rifles in their hands.

Pastor Jackson met them as they waded their mounts across Little Green Valley Creek. Walter Lambert walked slightly behind him, worry sketched on his face.

'Gentlemen.'

'Pastor.' Real put a finger to the brim of his hat.

'You look ill used, Mr Lee.'

Real ignored the comment about his battered features. 'Pearson Tate's as mean a gun hand as Arizona's ever seen, Pastor. He's got a bunch of men used to gun work, and they're coming here to clean the Assembly of Christ off this land. For good.'

'The good Lord will protect us,' Jackson said.

'Right now you'd better figure us your protection.' Real looked hard at Walt Lambert. 'Walt, you're a military man. You think some of your men could help us get ready for Tate?'

Jackson puffed up. 'Gentlemen. Today is the Sabbath. It

120

is not a day for work or fighting. The Assembly will hold services and we will rest, as the Lord says we must.'

Real heaved a sigh. 'When I was at VMI,' he said, 'we had a chaplain by the name of Leland Richards. He made sure we studied the Bible, as good soldiers should. And he had us learn from Ephesians, the sixth chapter and sixteenth verse. Do you know what it says, Pastor Jackson?'

Jackson ducked his head.

'. . . take up the full armor of God, that you may be able to resist in the evil day, and having done everything, to stand firm.' Real let the silence build. 'Sounds to me like God wants us to do for ourselves first and let Him pick up where we leave off. And that's what I intend to do.'

Real shot a glance at Walt Lambert. 'Tell me, Walt. How'd you set it up so a few men could stand off a company of mounted rifles?'

Lambert frowned and scuffed at the red-brown dirt with a booted toe.

'Come on, Walt. Gotta be done quick and dirty. And without giving the troop any advance warning.'

'Where will they come from?'

'If I were to guess, I'd say down the wagon track you dam builders laid from here to there. But Tate may be smarter than that. There's no telling.'

'Hmmm.'

'I'll say this. Things should look natural. People should be moving around, but never far from their cabins. They need to disappear when the first shot's fired.'

'I'll put wagons at the head of each street. Only four. Soon as we know where they're coming from, we tip the wagons on their sides and take cover.'

'We?' Real raised an eyebrow.

'We can at least help by tipping the wagons over. Those

121

big thick bottoms'll stop most everything short of a buffalo gun or a Gatling,' Lambert said, excitement showing in his voice.

'Good. Now,' Real turned his attention to Jackson. 'I reckon you'd better call your flock together, Pastor. They've got a right to know what's coming.'

Jackson nodded.

'You got anything to add, Tom? Finn?'

'Let's stop jawing,' Tom Easter said.

Sparrow ran from the willows lining the stream. 'They come,' he said.

13

'Shit.' Real spat. 'Walt, get those wagons set up. Tom, Finn, find yourselves some cover. Sparrow, where're they coming from?'

Sparrow waved his hand toward the wagon track leading north toward the dam site. 'Many riders, Real. Very many.'

'Get out of here. You'll do better from where they're not expecting you,' Real said.

Sparrow catfooted back into the willows. No flight of birds marked his passage.

'Pastor, you'd better see to your people. Keep them inside, lying on the floor. Pile up anything that may stop a bullet. Go!'

Tom Easter, Finn McBride, and Real Lee galloped into the cluster of cabins that was Respite. In a small corral, they laid their horses down and tied their legs to keep them there. Perhaps they'll be out of the line of fire. Good horses shouldn't get hurt just because men shoot at each other.

Walt Lambert and some Assembly men got two wagons tipped across the track at the north edge of Respite.

Real checked his pockets for extra shells, checked his

Frontier Colt and added a sixth bullet to its cylinder, and then checked the Colt Police model at his left hip. He strode to the overturned wagons. 'Get out of here,' he said to the Assembly men. 'Take cover. Keep outta sight.'

The men and boys scattered.

Real glanced at Tom and Finn. 'Dollar a day and found, eh?' he said. 'Reckon we're about to earn our pay. Y'all'd better find some cover away from the wagons. Best not get too bunched up.'

The sound of pounding hoofs came before Pearson Tate's riders showed.

'I've got the middle,' Real shouted, and jacked a shell into the breach of his Winchester.

The troop of gunmen came around a bend in the wagon track at a full run, pistols drawn and ready. Twenty men, for sure. Where'd the extras come from? Real had no time to ponder. 'God, I hate to do this,' he muttered, and shot the leading horse through the neck. It dropped as if shot between the eyes, throwing its rider into the dust.

Guns roared right and left. One more rider dropped.

As he levered and shot, levered and shot, levered and shot, Real saw a shadow slip from the junipers bordering the wagon track and leap up behind the last rider. The broad blade of a Bowie flashed in the early morning light, and the rider fell. Sparrow disappeared.

Four horses were down by the time Tate's riders started to split so they could surround the little town. Real Lee stepped out in front of the wagon blockade. He levered and shot. Another horse went down.

Pearson Tate rode in the center of the oncoming horde, with Tag Eidelbauer on his left and Amos Dwyer on his right. Eidelbauer threw his hands wide and tumbled from his horse, dead before he hit the ground. Then to

124

ground as the distant crack of a rifle sounded from the heights. Real grinned. Wolf Wilder and his one-in-a-thousand Winchester '73 were taking their toll of Tate's riders.

'God damn you, Real Lee,' Tate roared. He fired his six-gun as fast as he could cock the hammer and pull the trigger.

Real stood stock still as bullets whined around him. He knew a man on a running horse has little chance of hitting what he aims at. He laughed.

The riders spread out farther in a flanking movement. They fired six-guns as they rode, pouring lead into anything that looked like it might be hiding someone.

A bullet cut across the top of Real's shoulder. He ignored the wasp-like sting and the warm trickle that told him the grazing bullet had drawn blood. Without thinking, he counted the riders. Sixteen. Three without horses, thirteen mounted.

Dust flew. Hoofs thundered. Tate's riders slammed through Respite's meager defenses and galloped by the silent cabins, shooting as they rode. Most of the windows were oiled paper so the gunmen's bullets left small round holes. Here and there, panes shattered, adding the tinkle of falling glass to the cacophony.

Real slipped around the tipped wagon as Tate's riders flashed past. He pulled his Frontier Colt free and emptied it at the hurtling horsemen. None fell from his saddle. Real scrabbled in his pocket for shells to feed into his rifle. A bullet plowed into the wagon bed next to his hand. For a moment, he'd forgotten the riders whose horses were down. He dropped to the ground and searched for the source of the shot. Lightning's rifle cracked from behind the fallen log at the same time the sound of Wilder's shot came from the heights. One man threw his hands wide and fell over backwards. No one else moved.

'One more behind that juniper,' Lightning called. 'I can't get a bead on him.'

Real could hear the distinctive sounds of rifles coming from amidst the din of Tate's riders firing their six-guns. He wondered where Tom and Finn were, but couldn't locate their hiding places.

Tate's riders gathered on the far side of Respite. No one there to tip the wagon over to form a shield. All Real could do was wait for them to ride back. He whirled to meet the sound of pounding running feet. He held his Winchester waist high, muzzle pointed at the place where the runner would come around the wagon, and he almost pulled the trigger when Walt Lambert lunged into sight, a .50 caliber Sharps buffalo gun in his hands.

'You damn near got shot, Walt,' he said.

Lambert grinned. 'Figured maybe I could help out.'

'What can you hit with that cannon?'

'Squirrels at five hundred yards, men at a thousand.'

Real waved at the horsemen grouped on the far side of Respite. 'Take your pick,' he said. 'Those gunnies figure to kill the whole Assembly, and they knew it was gun work when they signed on. Have at it.'

Lambert nodded, set the big rifle on the side of the overturned wagon, and adjusted the rear sight. 'I make it about half a mile, Real. What do you think?'

'You set the sights, Walt. You know your gun.'

Lambert's Sharps .50 bellowed and a rider at the edge of Tate's milling bunch dropped from his saddle, bounced when he hit the ground, and lay still.

Another gunman swayed, clapping a hand to his belly, and slumped over his saddlehorn. The crack of Wilder's rifle came from the heights.

Finn McBride stepped from behind the southernmost cabin. 'Hey Tate,' he hollered. 'I never got to toss you one of these when you was over to the dam site.' He lit the fuse on a stick of dynamite with a cheroot, waited for it to burn down an inch or so, then lobbed it high and far towards Tate's riders.

'A quarter of a mile's farther than any man can throw a rock, much less a stick of dynamite,' Real muttered. 'What in Hell does he think he's doing?'

The dynamite hit, rolled, and went off in a massive shower of dirt and pebbles. Several of the outlaws horses went to bucking. Tate shouted. His men shouted. McBride shouted. Walt Lambert's Sharps bellowed. And another gunman fell.

Real started walking south. 'It's time we met Tate's men head on,' he said. Walt Lambert trotted over to take a place at Real's side. Lightning ran from his cover behind the log to take a place at Real's other side.

'You'd better have a short gun,' Real said to Walt, and handed him the Colt Police from his left hand holster.

'Thanks,' Walt said, and took the gun.

Tom Easter and Finn McBride waited at the south edge of the gaggle of Assembly cabins. They stepped out to make five men, line abreast.

'Pearson Tate,' Real hollered. Wolf Wilder joined the line. Sparrow stood up from where he'd hidden in the high grass.

'Seven of us, Tate,' Real shouted. 'And I count twelve of you. It's time we settled this once and for all. These folks got a right to be here, and you gunnies got no right to force them off their land. Fill your hands, you sons of bitches!'

Seven men in a skirmish line. Seven men with rifles in

127

their hands and six-guns in their belts. Seven men to face the hot lead of men who wanted them dead.

A loud voice sounded in the silence preceding the storm. 'Glory be to God and to his Son Jesus Christ!'

Pastor Eli Jackson pushed between Real Lee and Walt Lambert, holding his Bible high with his right hand. His shirt was torn and ragged, his pants looked thin at the knees, held up by a pair of mismatched suspenders, and his shoes looked much the worse for wear. But still he bore a dignity, a surety, the air of a man who has taken fate into his own hands.

Jackson walked in solemn silence toward Pearson Tate and his riders. Halfway between the seven men who protected Respite and the gunmen who wanted to annihilate the town, Jackson stopped. Facing Tate's men, he went to his knees. Carefully, he placed the Bible on the ground before him. Raising his hands in supplication to heaven, he began to recite the Lord's Prayer.

'Our Father who art . . .'

The women of the Assembly filtered through the line of seven men, led by Eli Jackson's wife. They knelt in a half circle behind him. Their voices joined Jackson's. 'Though I walk through the valley of the shadow of death,' they intoned.

The men and the children of the Assembly joined Jackson. The whole town knelt on the ground in front of Pearson Tate and his remaining gunmen, yet not a shot was fired.

'Amen,' the Assembly chorused at the end of the prayer.

After a moment, Jackson raised his voice again. 'Blessed are the poor in spirit. . . .' His flock joined in the recitation of the Beatitudes.

Walt Lambert turned to Real Lee. 'He's got it right, Real,' he said. 'Hang on to this for me.' He handed the Sharps .50 to Real. 'And thanks for the loan of the pistol.' Lambert returned the Colt Police Special to Real, then went to join the rest of the Assembly of Christ, kneeling on the ground.

'Blessed are the meek. . . .'

A horse splashed across the shallows of Little Green Valley Creek and thundered toward Respite at a gallop. Rolly Grieves, the Cibie rider, reined the horse in at the edge of town, slid out of his saddle, and ran toward the line of seven men. He came to a stop in front of Lightning.

'What's going on?' His question was nearly a shout.

Lightning shook his head. 'The pastor and the Assembly are out there fixing to get shot like pigs in a pen,' he said.

Rolly turned to watch.

'Blessed are the merciful. . . .'

Rolly stood unmoving for a long moment, then unbuckled his gunbelt and handed it to Lightning. 'If Ruth wants this, so do I.' He removed his hat and held it in his hand as he approached the kneeling Assembly. At the edge of the kneeling believers, he paused until he found Ruth Jackson, then went to kneel beside her. He put his hat on the ground.

Real shouted to be heard above the drone of the Assembly's recitation. 'What'll it be, Tate?'

One of the gunmen slid his rifle into its saddle scabbard and folded his hands on his saddlehorn. He walked his horse past the kneeling Assembly toward the line, now six.

'I don't want to kill helpless folks,' he said. 'If it's just the same with you, I'll be heading for Sonora. Got a Mexican girl there I'm partial to.'

'Hey Roy Bob. Wait up.' Two more riders peeled away from Tate's bunch and galloped after the first one.

'You Roy Bob Hill?' Real asked.

'I am.'

'Always heard you were a man of your word,' Real said. 'Ride on.'

Roy Bob put a finger to the brim of his hat in salute and turned his piebald toward the creek.

'Blessed are the peacemakers. . . .'

Pearson Tate shoved his rifle into its scabbard. 'Your day, Real Lee,' he called. 'We're pulling out.'

'Blessed are they who are persecuted for righteousness sake. . . .'

Real Lee watched Pearson Tate and his remaining riders as they circled Respite and rode north, apparently toward Payson. 'Tate's calling it off,' he said, 'but I reckon he doesn't figure things are over and done with. Not with Dywer and Skousen still riding with him.'

'Blessed are ye when men shall revile you, and persecute you, and say all manner of evil against you for my sake, for great is your reward in Heaven. Amen.' The Assembly stood as one and turned toward their town.

'Children, the Lord God has caused the angel of death to pass us by,' Jackson said. 'Praise the Lord.'

'Praise the Lord,' the Assembly echoed. They fell in behind their pastor, who led them toward the center of Respite.

Only six gunmen in Real Lee's line now, and they moved aside to let the Assembly pass. Walt Lambert stopped in front of Real Lee, his arm about the shoulders of a comely woman in her mid-twenties. 'Thank you, Real,' he said, 'and meet Emily, my wife.'

Real leaned the Sharps against his waist and raised his

hat. 'Pleased to meet you, ma'am. If I had a wife like yours, Walt, I'd stay right here in this town day and night.' He picked the Sharps up by the barrel. 'You'll want this.'

Lambert shook his head. 'I killed men today,' he said. 'I don't ever want to do that again. You keep the gun, Real. I'll not be using guns, ever.' He smiled. 'Emily tells me we're going to have a baby, Real. I don't want my son, or my daughter, whichever, to grow up in a place where every man has to wear a gun. Pastor Jackson is right about that.'

Real smiled and held out his hand. 'You've got more courage that just about any man I ever met,' he said. 'Proud to know you.'

Finn McBride stuck his hand out, too. 'That goes for me as well, Walt. Proud to know you.'

'Thanks, Finn.' Lambert shook hands with Real and Finn, then pulled something from his pocket. 'Actually, double thanks to you, Finn. Your dynamite uncovered this.' He held out a walnut-size bit of rock.

Finn took the rock and turned it over in his palm. He looked at Walt. 'Copper?'

Lambert nodded. 'I sent young Hugh Freelock to Globe City to file claims.'

'Claims?'

'I reckon every family in Respite needs a claim if we're going to make a copper mine work. Better for us than silver or gold, I reckon. Never heard of a copper rush.'

'You're gonna need money, I'd say.'

'No rush, once we've got legal claims.'

Real nodded. 'That could be right.' He held out a hand and Finn put the rock in it. Real turned the piece of ore over and over. 'Hmmm.' He handed the ore back to Lambert. 'When you need money, come see me. I'll most likely be in Payson.'

'I'll do that.' This time, Lambert put his hand out.

Real shook it. '*Vaya con Dios*,' he said.

'You, too.' Lambert and Emily hurried after the Assembly. Rock of Ages echoed across the flats as the Sabbath meeting began.

14

'Tom,' Real said. 'I reckon things in Respite will settle down now. I'll be pulling out as soon as I get my gear together.'

'Be obliged if you all would help me check the dead and carry them to that gully so we can cave that overhang on to them,' Tom said. 'Then we can settle up. Dollar a day and found.'

'Shoulda gone about this a little slower,' Finn said. 'Dollar a day's not going to amount to much.' He grinned. 'Glad none of the Assembly died, though.'

'Let's get them dead gunnies gathered up,' Wilder said. 'Sparrow, come with me.'

'Lightning,' said Real. 'You and me've been a bit of a team through this, maybe we should haul dead men together, too.'

By noon, the horsemen had buried nine of Tate's Big Johney Gulch gunmen. One was still alive. They turned him over to the Assembly. Four of the horses were down, six others got rounded up. They took the horses and the gunmen's gear into Respite.

'Pastor,' Tom Easter said, 'those riders we buried will have no need of these horses or this gear. I reckon you could keep them here.'

'The good Lord has smiled upon us in our day of trial,' Jackson said. 'We will accept the horses and their tack, but nothing else.'

'Would you happen to have a gunnysack?' Easter asked.

'We do. Jonathan. A gunnysack from the stores, if you please.'

A youngster ran off and soon returned with a sack, which he handed to Easter.

'Thank you, son,' he said. He dumped the dead outlaw's six-guns into the sack. 'We'll take care of these, and their rifles.'

An awkward silenced followed.

'We'll be leaving then,' Tom Easter said at last. He, Finn McBride, and Real Lee got their horses from the corral. Lightning retrieved his from a thicket of willows near the creek. Wilder and Sparrow struck out on foot.

As the horsemen rode to the edge of Respite, Rolly Grieves called after them. 'Mr Easter. Oh, Mr Easter.' He ran to catch up with them. 'Mr Easter, just so you know, Mr Brockman's daughter Sybil come back from St. Louis. She's going to take Mr Brockman to San Francisco for doctoring, and she's put Ace Duggan in charge of the Cibie.'

'That's good. Ace will keep things going all right. Thanks for telling us, son. And what'll you do?'

Rolly ducked his head. He got his gunbelt from Lightning and held it out. 'Take this, Mr Easter. Do with it what you'll do with those other guns. I'll do whatever Pastor Jackson says. I'll be the man he'll let marry Ruth, or die trying.'

Easter chuckled. 'You do that, boy. Help build up this town.'

*

The four horsemen and two youngsters gathered at the campsite atop the hogback overlooking Respite. They took down the lean-tos and Wilder's wickiup, and cleaned the area. When they finished, only the three rocks that held the dutch oven over the coals remained.

Tom Easter dug a poke from his saddle-bags. 'Time to pay up,' he said. 'I told Mr Whiting that thirty days pay was the least we'd go for, so each of you has three eagles coming.'

'Two for me,' Lightning said.

'Can't bitch about thirty dollars,' Wilder said. 'Short of cash these days at the Flying W.' He held out his hand. 'Three gold eagles it is, then.'

Easter put the coins in Wilder's hand. 'As always, Wolf, things go better when you're around.'

'Hell, Tom. Just doing the job,' he said.

'And you, Sparrow. Proud to make your acquaintance.' Easter gave three gold eagles to Sparrow.

'My thanks, Tom Easter,' Sparrow said. Then he turned to Wilder and handed him the money.

Easter raised an eyebrow but said nothing. He paid McBride and Real Lee, and gave two eagles to Lightning Brewster. 'I reckon that evens things up,' he said. 'Now. I'm headed for Holbrook, and Gallup after that. Anyone riding that way?'

'I'll ride with Wilder,' Finn McBride said. 'Stop by the Flying W for some of Blessing's good cooking, then up through Camp Kinishba and Ponderosa to Paradise and the Rafter P.'

'Lilywhite's in Payson,' Real Lee said. 'I've a mind to put my feet under her table, maybe for quite a spell.'

'Real Lee?' Lightning didn't look at Real, just scrubbed at the dirt with the toe of a boot. 'Real, I'd admire to ride with you, if you'll let me.'

Real smiled. 'Son, you're welcome,' he said.

They stood a moment longer, looking down at Respite. The Sabbath meeting was over and the Assembly had gone back to their cabins. Smoke rose from a dozen chimneys. Peace and quiet reigned.

'*Adios amigos,*' Easter said. He reined his black stallion east toward Pleasant Valley and Holbrook.

Wilder, Sparrow, and Finn McBride turned south. Wilder's brindle grulla stood shoulder to shoulder with McBride's white appaloosa, and Sparrow followed on his little gray mare. 'Sparrow,' Wilder said, 'You're on scout.'

Sparrow gigged the mare and rode on ahead. At the brow of the hill, he turned and raised a hand to Lightning, then dropped off the hill and out of sight.

'Reckon we'd better move along, Lightning,' Real Lee said.

'We going back to Payson?'

'I am. You can go where you please.'

'I'll ride along.'

'Come on, then.'

Real and Lightning rode north, then west. They camped for the night in Rough Valley and approached Payson as the sun neared its zenith in a cloudless sky.

'You reckon that Tate feller's here?' Lightning said.

'Maybe.'

'You reckon he'll pull iron on ya?'

'Maybe.'

'You reckon you can beat him? Kill him?'

'Maybe. Or him me.'

'Shee-it.'

'I'm getting almighty tired of gun work,' Real said. 'The days of the quick draw and fast shot are fading. No doubt you'll still be around when men don't have to carry guns all the time. Maybe I won't, but you will.'

They walked their horses up Beeline and turned on to Main. Webber's Livery stood on the left, door to the big barn standing open. 'We'll board the horses here,' Real said, and reined Sorry into the barn.

'What can I do for you gents?'

Real gave the old man a hard look as he dismounted. Lightning sat easy on Patches, but his eyes flicked here and there, looking for any sign of danger in the gloom of the big barn.

'Name's Glidden,' the old man said. 'Henry Glidden. Folks used to call me Speakeasy on account I'm always talking, but now it's just Speak, like I was a mutt or sumpin. Reckon you'll be wanting to put up them hosses. Whaddaya figure? A week? No? Just today?'

'What's the damage for a month, Speak?' Real said.

'A whole month?'

'To start with.'

'Well. Well. Well. Usually it's a dollar a day and found, grain extry,' Speak said. 'But some like Miss Lilywhite board hosses kinda permanent like and they pays fifteen bucks a month. Yeah. Fifteen bucks'll do it, with hay.'

'Quart of oats a day?'

'Two bits.'

'How about a dollar a week for oats, then?'

Speak rubbed at the white stubble on his chin. 'We-e-ell, OK. Being as you'll pay up front if you want to board them hosses.'

'You got it.'

Real dug in his pocket for the three eagles Easter had given him. 'Toss me an eagle, Lightning,' he said. He put his three eagles and the one from Lightning in Speak's

137

hand. 'That'll be two cartwheels back, Speak, if you please.'

'I'm gonna need y'all's names,' Speak said.

'Gabriel Lee and Lightning Brewster.'

'Lightning of God Brewster,' Lightning said.

'That's a helluva moniker, young'un,' Speak said. 'Hang on.' He disappeared into a room built on to the inside of the barn and reappeared a moment later with two silver dollars. 'There you go, Real Lee,' he said, a slight smirk on his face. He'd heard of Real Lee no doubt.

Real handed him Sorry's reins. 'Hold him while I get my gear.' He pulled his Colt Frontier from its holster and added a sixth bullet to its cylinder.

'Expectin' trouble?' Speak said.

'Pays to be ready,' Real said.

Lightning handed over Patches' reins, put another bullet in his Remington Army, then removed his bedroll from behind the cantle and snaked his Winchester from its scabbard. Bedroll under his left arm, Winchester in his left hand, Lightning left his right hand free. He nodded to Real. 'Ready when you are,' he said.

Real had bedroll, saddle-bags, Winchester, and Ithaca shotgun, but still managed to keep his gun hand free. 'To the Stockman,' he said, and strode from the barn.

Maybe they saw Real and Lightning ride into town. Maybe someone ran from the livery to tell them Real Lee was in town. Maybe the reasons didn't matter. Halfway between the livery and the Stockman Hotel, two shots sounded and Real Lee went down.

15

As Real collapsed, Lightning's Remington filled his hand. His first shot sent a rifleman's hat flying. An instant later, his second hit the man on the point of the chin, tore off the left side of his jaw, and plowed into his neck, blowing a chunk out of his jugular vein. The gunman threw up his arms and arched back, falling behind the false front of the millinery shop he'd mounted. A rifle clattered down the steep roof incline, followed by the gunman's body, which plopped to the ground atop the rifle, lifeless.

Lightning's attention had already shifted elsewhere. He sent lead flying after the disappearing form of a second gunman, who staggered, then kept on running and disappeared behind the buildings of Main Street. No one on the street moved. People stood in place, frozen by the brazen bushwhacking of Real Lee, who now lay in the middle of the street, blood leaking from a bullet hole in his back.

Lightning stood statue-still for a long moment. When no other gunman showed, he knelt by Real, his gun held ready. Real breathed. He was alive.

'Hey, you,' Lightning shouted. 'Hey, you with the team.'

Lightning's shout unfroze the citizens of Payson. The

teamster hurried to Lightning's side. 'Whatcha want, kid?' he asked.

'Help me get this man to the hotel. Miss Lilywhite's room.' Lightning holstered his Remington. Others gathered, and Lightning asked two of them to carry his and Real's bedrolls, the rifles and shotgun, and the saddlebags.

Jorge Valenzuela stood at the door of the hotel when the group arrived. He led them through the lobby and up the stairs. The door to Lilywhite's room was already open, and Lilywhite took over the moment they entered with Real.

'Put him on the bed. Jorge, you get the cook downstairs to boil some water. Lightning, run to the barbershop and get Kendall Johnson. He's the closest thing to a doctor in Payson.

Lightning pounded down the stairs and ran to the barbershop. 'You Kendal Johnson?' he shouted at the man stropping a straight-edge razor.

'Yeah. So what?'

Lightning swallowed hard so he could talk about Real. 'My friend Real Lee got backshot. He needs your help. Miss Lilywhite's asking that you come.'

'Miss Lilywhite? I'll be right there.'

'She's in room twenty-two at the Stockman. You fix that man, y'hear.'

Johnson gave Lightning a sharp look. 'I ain't no doctor,' he said. 'All I can do is what I learned in the war and what I've done since. I'll do what I know to do. Other than that, I can't make any promises.'

'Well, you go on over,' Lightning said. Then he added, 'Please.'

*

Real Lee heard things first. The low buzz of voices. The clink of metal on china. The swish of skirts as a woman walked across the room. He heard it all through a haze of pain. Someone had taken a sledgehammer to his skull, and then pushed a red hot poker into his back.

'The shot in the back must have hit first,' a man said. 'I got the bullet out. Another bullet creased his skull. That knocked him unconscious, but I don't think it cracked the bone. Nice part in his hair, though.'

'I ain't dead,' Real mumbled.

'Real. Real. Darling.' Soft fingers touched his brow. He pried an eyelid open far enough to see Lilywhite leaning over him with concern on her face and two little worry wrinkles between her eyebrows.

'This heaven?' Real asked.

Lilywhite smiled. 'No, dear.'

'Thought it might be. Angels being here and all. Where's Lightning?'

'Here, Real.'

'Who done it?'

'They were two gunmen, Real. I only got one. Wanted to see you were OK before I go hunting the other one.'

'I'll live, I reckon. Be up 'fore long.'

'They call the one I shot Lightfoot Billy,' Lightning said.

'Never heard of him.'

'*Señor*,' Jorge said. 'It is well to hear you speak. I have seen this Lightfoot in Payson. He often, how do you say, *roncear* at the saloon called Branding Iron.'

'The Branding Iron?'

'*Sí.*'

'Kyle Benford owns the Branding Iron,' Lilywhite said. 'He's my competition and he owns many of the buildings in town.'

141

Real tried to lever himself up. 'Damn, that hole in my back feels a mile wide,' he said through clenched teeth. 'Lightning, Jorge, gimme a hand. A man thinks better sitting up.'

'I dug that bullet out of you, Mr Lee. All I can say is you're lucky that .44-40 shell was off kilter. Bullet stopped dead up against a rib, right next to your backbone. Shoulda busted on through, but it didn't. Don't know why.'

'So other than a new part in my hair and a little hole in my back, I'm OK. That what you're saying?'

'It is.'

Jorge and Lightning helped Real to sit up. Lilywhite fluffed feather pillows and placed them where the wound in Real's back would not come against them.

'Damn,' Real said. 'Sitting up makes a man's head hurt.'

'My ma always made willow bark tea,' Lightning said. 'Indians use it to get rid of pain.'

'What kind of willow?' Lilywhite asked.

'Ma used red willows. That's all they was.'

'Could you ride over to Fossil Creek? Willows grow there,' Lilywhite said. 'Strip some bark and we'll try it. Can't do any harm.'

'Be right back,' Lightning said, and thundered down the stairs.

'Bruises and bullet holes. Not much to say for a man who's past thirty,' Real said. He looked at the scarred hands in his lap. 'Bruises and bullet holes.'

'Bruises heal, darling. And bullet holes grow into scars,' Lilywhite said. 'To me they're testimony that you always try to help the weak and take the right side of things. Those settlers didn't deserve to be driven from their homes. You and your friends stepped in. Now they can build in peace.'

'Dollar a day and found,' Real said. 'No more than that.'

Lilywhite laughed. 'And when did you start doing gun work for a cowboy's wage?'

Real stared out the window, seeing nothing. 'Pearson Tate's still out there. So's Amos Dwyer and Peg Skousen, although Peg owes me for not killing him on the hogback.'

'Right now you should be thinking about recovering from beatings and shootings,' Lilywhite scolded. 'No one's going to break into my room. Not with Jorge watching.'

'Were people to think I was barely hanging on, someone might sneak up here with a shotgun. Anyone's bound to make a mistake, sometimes even Jorge.'

'I've done all I can,' Kendall Johnson said. 'From now on, it's just a matter of sleep and lots of good red meat, lots of it.'

Real gave the barber a wan smile. 'For someone who's not a doctor, you do right well, Kendall Johnson. I'm beholden to you. But if you could do me one more favor, I'd appreciate it.'

Johnson nodded. 'Do what I can,' he said.

'You make out that I may not live, could you? You did everything you could, but the bullet was too deep and the head shot busted my skull. Don't say much. Just feel real sorry for me, OK?'

'I can do that.' Johnson smiled, like deceit was right up his alley.

'Good man. You can cut my hair when I'm back on my feet.' Real grinned. 'Judging from your doctoring, I'd say you're a helluva hair cutter too.'

'Miss Lilywhite, I'll be getting back to the barbershop then.'

143

'Thank you, Kendall.' Lilywhite took his hand in both of hers, and left a gold eagle behind.

Johnson started. He opened his mouth to protest, but Lilywhite put a finger to her lips, shushing him.

'You helped a man who is very dear to me,' she said. 'Thank you.' She showed Johnson to the door.

After the barber left, Real said, 'Now. We need to get ready for visitors.'

Lightning brought the willow bark back and Lilywhite steeped it in hot water to make a bitter brew that seemed to relieve Real Lee's headache. Lilywhite sent Lightning out again, this time for two roast beef dinners from Maggie at Ma Becker's.

'If anyone asks, the beef's for you and Jorge,' she said. 'And ask Maggie to make up some beef broth for Real.'

Lightning told Maggie what he wanted in a voice loud enough for all six of Ma Becker's customers to hear. 'Miss Lilywhite'll pay you,' he said.

Jorge opened the door when Lightning kicked it. He grinned at Lightning, who juggled two large plates heaped with roast beef, mashed potatoes smothered in gravy, chunks of baked squash, and a mound of green peas. A large coffee pot hung from his right arm and a similar pot of beef broth from his left. 'Don't just stand there, Jorge, help. My arms are about to fall off. Come on. Give a feller a break, would you.'

Jorge barked a laugh, but took the two plates from Lightning. '*Bueno*,' he said. '*Señor Real tiene mucho hambriento.*'

'Thanks, Lightning,' Real said. 'My head's decided to stay on my neck and my stomach's decided those gunmen sliced my throat instead of just shooting me.'

'Come, darling. The food will get cold,' Lilywhite said.

Lightning watched Real wolf the food, then made a decision. 'Be back shortly,' he said. He stepped into the dimly lit hallway and walked to the head of the stairs. He drew his Remington and checked the loads and the action. Smooth and positive. By habit, he added the sixth shell to the cylinder. He took a deep breath, holstered the Remington, and walked down the stairs to the lobby. The clerk looked up, gave him a friendly smile, and went back to his ledger. Lightning let himself out of the front door.

Twilight hid many of the blemishes of Payson. The shops stood dark and sober. A wagon clattered east on Main and turned south on Beeline. A lantern glowed in the livery, and light spilled over the batwings of the Branding Iron. The tinkle of a piano seemed to be coming from the Ox Bow further down the street. Lightning took another deep breath and strode toward the Branding Iron. The time had come to shake the tree and see what kind of apples fell.

He pushed the batwings inwards and stepped into the saloon. A glance showed him the layout. Bar down the right-hand side of the long room, backed in the center by a large mirror. Three men in working range clothes stood about midway down the bar, hats tipped back and shot glasses in hand. A bottle stood in front of them, uncorked and more than halfway gone.

The tables seemed to have no rhyme to their placement. A card game filled one table with the house gambler dealing. Working doves sat by their targets in chairs pulled up from other tables. The men didn't even look up from their cards when Lightning walked in.

A dove came down the stairway that probably led to rooms on the second floor. She plastered on a smile when

145

she saw Lightning. He gave her a hard look and she changed directions, going over to watch the card game. Lightning went to the bar.

One table sat away from the rest, far in the back of the room, shadowed by the stair landing. At the moment, it was empty.

Lightning bought a whiskey. He carried it over to the card game and stood watching, the drink in his left hand. He ignored the dove.

'Damn.' The card player wore the clothing of a small-time rancher, or maybe even a sodbuster, if such lived anywhere near Payson. 'Can't never get a decent hand,' he grumbled. He laid his cards face down on the table. 'I'm out. Shit.'

'Too bad, Sloan,' the house gambler said. 'The missus won't like you coming home without the pay for that load of hay you left at the livery. Want I should loan you enough for another hand? See if you can make that money back?'

Sloan looked at the gambler, longing in his eyes. Then the fire went out. 'Nah. Luck ain't in my favor,' he said. He stood, heaved a sigh, and slouched away.

'Thanks for the drink, Mr Sloan,' a dove called.

'Do you mind, Shark?' Lightning asked.

'Help yourself,' the gambler said.

'Game?'

'Seven-card stud.'

'Stakes?'

Shark looked at the other two players. 'Bret? Slim? Dollar stakes?'

'Upping the stakes, eh? Your game, then. I'm out.' The man who spoke wore the leathered look of a man who herded cattle. He patted the knee of the dove sitting next to him. 'Gotta get back to the B Bar anyway.' He stood.

'Gentlemen. Ladies. Another day, then.'

'I'll be here anytime you want to play, Bret,' the gambler said.

Lightning took the last eagle from his dollar-a-day-and-found money and put it on the table. 'Break this?' he said.

Shark traded ten silver dollars for the eagle. 'Short game?' he asked.

Lightning grinned, and set the glass of whiskey on the table. 'We'll see,' he said. He sat so he could watch the empty back table. He pushed his Stetson back on his head. 'Deal,' he said.

By the time Pearson Tate showed, Lightning's stack of silver dollars had grown to twenty-five, and the players at the table watched him with careful eyes. He seemed nonchalant and carefree, but somehow won more than he lost.

Tate took a seat at the empty table. A few minutes later, a short wiry man came down the stairs and joined Tate. Lightning recognized him as one of the riders who'd attacked Respite, but didn't know his name. 'Who's those at the back table?' he asked the gambler. 'Seems I've seen them somewhere before.'

'Ever been to Big Johney Gulch?'

'No.'

'The big one's Pearson Tate. He rides high at Big Johney.'

'Yeah? How 'bout the little guy?'

The gambler gave Lightning a sharp look. 'Little, but tough as boiled owl. That's Dwyer. Amos Dwyer. He came north from Texas with Tate.'

Lightning nodded. 'Deal me out,' he said, pocketed the stack of cartwheels, and left the whiskey untouched on the table. 'You can have that booze, if you want it,' he said to

147

the dove standing behind the gambler. 'I never touch the stuff.'

As Lightning walked toward the rear of the saloon, a man dressed in immaculate pearl-gray frock coat, white high-collar shirt with a peach cravat held by a large gold nugget stick pin, and gray striped trousers came through a door nearly hidden by the stairway. The man's face had a hint of cruelty but was soft around the jawline.

'Evening, Ben,' Tate said. The small wiry man's restless eyes noticed Lightning the moment he started toward the back table. He nudged Tate.

'You'll be Pearson Tate,' Lightning said.

'That's right.'

'You'll be the man who had my partner Real Lee bush-whacked. I killed one of the shooters, name of Lightfoot Billy, the othern got away. I only grazed him. People say Lightfoot Billy liked to drink at the Branding Iron. You hang out here. I'm thinking you put Billy up to that back-shooting job.'

'Real Lee's backshot?' Surprise was plain on Tate's face, but the fancy man he'd called Ben smirked.

'Backshot but not dead. If he was dead, I'd shoot first and then ask questions.' Lightning stopped a couple of steps from the table. 'I been thinking,' he said, looking at the fancy man. 'Real Lee got waylaid outside Respite. You did that, Tate. Then he was locked in a root cellar, hanging from the ceiling by chains. While he was there, he got beat twice, once by the butcher I shot through the shoulder, and once by a man he called Ben Seffleck.'

Lightning stared at the fancy man with hard eyes. 'I reckon you're the man known hereabouts as Kyle Benford, but I figure Tate got it right. You're Ben. Ben Seffleck.'

Lightning stood ready.

Seffleck smirked. 'Once I was Ben Seffleck,' he said. 'Now I'm Kyle Benford. This is my town. I have no one to fear, so I never carry arms. Shoot me, young gunnie, and people will lynch you for killing an unarmed man.'

'Pearson Tate,' Lightning said. 'You said things wasn't finished with Real when you rode out of Respite. I'm here to finish them. If you can hold your head up in the morning, I'll be waiting on Frontier Street two hours after sunrise. If you don't show, I'll come hunting.'

16

The day dawned clear and cloudless, though there was a bite of frost in the air. Lightning rose from his bed of hay at the livery as the roosters around town began to crow. He didn't tell Real Lee he'd called out Pearson Tate. He didn't even tell Miss Lilywhite, well, especially not Miss Lilywhite. He used the two-holer behind the livery corral, then pumped a basin of water to wash up with. Dear Lord, the water was cold, but Lightning made a good job of it.

Lightning got his gun-cleaning gear from his saddle-bags, patted Patches on the way past, and sat down on a bench to make sure his Remington Army was ready for the day.

Carefully, he emptied the cartridges into his hat, then broke the gun down. He uncorked a little bottle of gun oil from his kit and dribbled a bit on a 2-inch square of cloth. He shoved the cloth into the barrel and stuffed it through to the breech with a short rod. He repeated the process half a dozen times, then used the oily cloth to wipe down each part of the gun.

He corked the oil bottle and put it away, then wiped all the gun parts, including the bullets, with a clean cloth.

After reassembling the Remington, he stood, put it in

150

its holster, and drew and dry-fired the gun. He wasn't trying for speed, just getting his hand accustomed the motions of drawing and firing.

Lightning's stomach growled. Time for breakfast at Ma Becker's. He reloaded the Remington and holstered it.

'Morning, kid,' Speakeasy called from one of the stalls.

'Morning.' Lightning left the livery and walked west on Main Street to Ma Becker's restaurant. People and wagons were just beginning to move about.

'Give me steak and eggs, Maggie,' he called as he took the only empty table.

'I ain't giving you nothing, kid,' Maggie called back. 'You'll pay, just like regular customers.'

Lightning laughed. 'With you ramrodding the place, I wouldn't think of freeloading.'

The steak came oozing red juices. Lightning wondered whose red blood would ooze on Frontier Street. He ate with gusto, shoving meat and egg into his mouth as fast as he could chew and swallow. In moments, he pushed the empty plate away.

'Got any apple pie,' he asked Maggie when she came after the plate.

Maggie gave him a funny look. 'Apple pie? At breakfast?'

'Who knows? May be the last apple pie I ever eat.'

'A piece or two left over from last night,' Maggie said. 'Cold, though.'

'Some cream to top it?'

'Got that.'

'If you please.' Lightning asked as politely as he knew how.

'More coffee?'

Lightning nodded, and when the pie came, he ate it

slowly, chewing each bite and savoring the tartness of the apples through the sweet of the sugar and the smoothness of the cream that topped the big slice. Apple pie and coffee. A fitting end to an ample last meal, if that was what this breakfast turned out to be.

What about Pearson Tate? Lightning couldn't figure the gunman out. His gun was bought and paid for, yet didn't seem to be the sneak-around-and-shoot-in-the-back kind. Lightning was ready. He would face a man he didn't know across thirty feet of dusty street. But always before, others had pushed Lightning. This time, he was doing the pushing. And he had no idea what Pearson Tate would do when he came to Frontier Street, but come he would.

By the time Lightning finished the pie and drank his coffee, the sun had climbed nearly two hours into the sky. He dropped a silver dollar on the table for the meal and one for Maggie. He hitched his gunbelt into a comfortable position on his hips. Then he went out to meet Pearson Tate.

Lightning walked west on Main. People stepped aside to let him pass. A wagon rumbled east toward Beeline, a sodbuster and his skinny wife on the high seat. Lightning turned north on Frontier. Men lined the street on both sides. Word of the morning gunfight had spread, bringing the usual gaggle of onlookers fascinated by other people's blood. Let them look. Things would be over in a few seconds. Lightning walked fifty feet into Frontier Street, then turned to face Main, feet spread shoulder-width apart, arms folded, and hat brim pulled low to shade his eyes.

The onlookers seemed to hold their breath. No one spoke. They fidgeted as they waited, but made little sound. A hawk screamed from somewhere high in the eastern sky.

Lightning waited, his mind blank. Reactions settled gun-fights, and his were better than most.

He stood in the middle of the street, relaxed but alert. He paid no attention to the spectators. He didn't care if people liked to watch other people die. His ears picked up the creak of saddle leather and the sound of a walking horse; no, two horses. Pearson Tate reined his blaze-faced bay into Frontier Street, followed by the short wiry man who'd sat by him at the back table in the Branding Iron.

Lightning's eyes narrowed. Otherwise, he didn't move.

Pearson stopped the bay and sat with his hands on the saddlehorn, looking at Lightning. A slight smile touched his lips.

'Pearson Tate!'

Real Lee stood at the side of the street, supported by Jorge Valenzuela.

'Tate, I got a hole in my back and a crease in my head, but I'll not have my friends doing my work,' Real said. He shrugged off Jorge's arm and walked stiffly to Lightning's side. 'I'm a walking wreck, Tate, but I reckon I can pull a gun. Lightning here's the fastest man I ever saw with a sixshooter. You'd never clear leather against him. With me, at least you'll have a fighting chance.'

Real shifted his attention to the other rider. 'Amos, you're quicker'n most, but Jorge over there and Lightning here will make sure you don't butt in on this business between Tate and me.'

Tate's smile widened. 'Real Lee. You about through jawing?'

'This ain't no time for conversation,' Real said.

'Let me say just one thing.'

Real's voice turned hard. 'Have your say, Tate.'

'I got hired to put a scare into a bunch of god-bothering sodbusters,' Tate said. 'We tried scaring them and we tried burning them out. Nothing worked.'

'So you went after them with guns.'

'How many of those settlers did we shoot, Real?'

Real thought for a moment. 'None,' he said.

Tate said, 'See?'

'Yeah.'

'I coulda killed you, Real, instead of giving you a few smacks. That said, I don't cotton to what the butcher and Kyle Benford did to you.'

'Kyle Benford?'

'Yeah. You'd know him as Ben Seffleck.'

'So where's all this jawing going?'

'I told you it wasn't over between us, Real, and I was hot under the collar when I said it. Men I'd hired went down under your guns. But that was before Benford had you bushwhacked. I don't go for shooting a man in the back. If you'll agree, I'll leave. Me'n Amos'll go back to Big Johney. Let bygones be bygones.'

Real and Lightning stood ready.

'What say?' Tate asked, his hands still relaxed on the saddlehorn.

Glass tinkled as a rifle barrel broke a pane from a window of the Branding Iron. Pearson Tate lifted the reins and would have touched the bay with his spurs, but a bullet knocked him from the saddle.

'You lousy bastard,' a frenzied voice shouted. 'I paid you good money—'

Bullets from the guns of Real Lee, Lightning Brewster, Amos Dwyer, and Jorge Valenzuela crashed through the window, but didn't seem to have hit the shooter. Maniacal laughter came from inside the Branding Iron.

'I'll get him,' Lightning shouted, darted up Frontier

154

Street, and skidded around the corner.

Real Lee knelt by Pearson Tate. 'Jorge. Amos. Come help.'

Tate struggled to rise, then fell again to the street.

'You hang in there, Pearson. Don't you die,' Real said. He raised his voice. 'Someone get Kendall Johnson.'

A man ran off toward the barbershop.

'Need something to plug that hole,' he muttered. 'Gotta stop the bleeding.'

'*Señor*,' Jorge said, 'here is my own *panuelo*.'

'*Gracias, amigo*,' Real said. He took the bandana, wadded it up, and poked it into the bullet hole in Tate's back, low and to one side. 'Help get this man to the hotel,' Real called. Townsmen carried the barely conscious Tate to the Stockman. Lilywhite already had a key when the men arrived. 'Number eleven,' she said. They carried Tate up the stairs and through the open door to room eleven. Real Lee climbed the stairs with laborious steps, once more leaning on Jorge.

Kendall Johnson ran into the lobby.

'Up here,' Real called.

The barber rushed past Real and Jorge, on up the stairs, and into the room. Real followed at a much slower pace.

Silence greeted Real as he entered room eleven. No one rushed around. No one shouted orders. No one.

'Pearson?' Real's voice came out subdued. He looked at Kendall Johnson, a question in his eyes.

Johnson merely shook his head.

'Shit.' Real's curse was almost a whisper. He went to the bed where Pearson Tate lay on his side. A sheet covered him and his breathing was so shallow Real could hardly see the rise and fall of the covering. Tate's pallid face wore a sheen of perspiration. He moaned as each breath left his body.

'Bullet took out a kidney,' Johnson said in a low voice. 'Probably tore his guts to pieces, too. Ain't nothing I can do, Real. I ain't no doctor, but I don't reckon there's one in the whole territory who could save him.'

'Shit.'

Real put a hand on Tate's shoulder. 'Pearson Tate,' he said. 'You took the wrong turn out of Big Johney Gulch, but no man should die from a bullet in the back. We'll find Benford or Seffleck or whatever he calls himself, and we'll deal with him. Trust me.'

Somehow Tate raised a hand to cover Real's. He didn't say anything, and little moans still came from deep inside his chest. He put a tiny bit of pressure on Real's hand. Then Tate's hand went limp and dropped to the bed. With a long exhalation, Pearson Tate gave his last moan and died.

'Shit.' Real reached over to close Tate's staring eyes. 'Shee-it,' he repeated.

Kendall Johnson took over. 'I reckon I'm the closest thing to an undertaker this burg has,' he said.

Real went to the window overlooking Main. 'Us who do gun work expect to die by the gun,' he said. 'But no gun man deserves to be shot in the back.'

A rumble of voices came from the direction of the Branding Iron. Lightning Brewster appeared, holding his Remington cocked and its muzzle jammed into the soft flesh below Ben Seffleck's jaw. Amos Dwyer shoved the barrels of a sawed-off shotgun against Seffleck's back as he walked a step behind. The wiry man's face was a mask of hate.

Most of the male population of Payson followed the two gunmen and their prisoner. Farmers. Teamsters. Cowboys. Merchants. Hangers-on. And behind them came the boys.

The crowd shouted, waved their fists in the air, and danced themselves into a frenzy.

Real Lee left room eleven. 'Come along, Jorge,' he said.

Jorge glanced at Lilywhite. '*Con permisso.*' She nodded, and Jorge left with Real.

They reached the door of the Stockman just as Lightning and Dwyer pushed Seffleck up on to the porch.

'Found him hiding in the storeroom,' Lightning said.

'Pears?' Dwyer asked.

'Pearson died not five minutes ago,' Real said.

'Son. Of. A. Bitch.' Dwyer punctuated each word with a jab of the shotgun barrels into Seffleck's back.

Seffleck squealed like a little girl.

Men crowded into the lobby of the hotel as Real, Lightning, Jorge, and Dwyer escorted Seffleck inside. Word of Pearson's death rippled through their ranks.

'Sumbitch backshot that cowboy.'

'Get a rope. We'll have us a necktie party.'

'Yeah! A necktie party. That's what this town needs. Goldam backshooter.'

Seffleck went to his knees before Real Lee. Tears streaked his cheeks. 'Gabriel Lee. We were both cadets at VMI. We were comrades. We were on the field of battle together, you and me. Together. Don't let these crazies kill me. I'm too valuable. I don't deserve to die. I . . . I. . . .'

Real looked down on Seffleck, his face impassive. He held up his hands. Gradually the shouting died down. Seffleck sniffled.

'Gentlemen,' Real said. 'Ben Seffleck shot a man dead from behind. But it's not the first time. He backshot a comrade in arms during the battle of New Market. I was there. He hired Lightfoot Billy to shoot me, too. I've got the hole in my back to prove it.

157

'String the sumbitch up.' The shout came from just outside the front door.

Real held his hands up again. 'Seffleck probably deserves to die. But think on this. If we string him up, we're no better than him.'

'Whatcha gonna do, then?'

'Payson's a growing town. People learn we do things right here, and they'll move to this town to live, raise families, build farms, run stores, dig mines, that kind of stuff.'

'So what? Stringing that lilyliver up's the thing to do, I swear.'

'Wait. Wait.' Real took a deep breath. 'Let me send my friend Lightning Brewster to Globe City to get Sheriff Reynolds. They could be back in a week or ten days. If the law says he dies, then he'll die.'

'Might be someone breaks him out. We ain't got no jail-house.'

Real looked at the faces in the crowd. He had them talking now. The fever to hang Seffleck didn't burn as bright. 'I know where to keep him,' he said. 'I spent some time there myself. And with Amos Dwyer and Jorge Valenzuela on guard, Seffleck won't be going anywhere. Trust me.'

Lightning arrived back from Globe City exactly nine days later. With him rode Sheriff Gill Reynolds and Justice R.B. McCabe. The justice called a jury of Payson's citizens and they listened to Dwyer, Lightning, Real, and the big man called the Butcher, then they all said Ben Seffleck was guilty.

Justice McCabe smacked his gavel on one of Ma Becker's tables. 'This court finds you, Benford Seffleck, guilty of murdering Pearson Tate by rifle shot to his back.

You will be taken by Sheriff Reynolds to Globe City and from there to the Territorial Prison in Yuma, where you will spend the rest of your natural life.' He smacked the gavel again.

The sheriff and the justice left Payson with Seffleck, hands bound, in the early morning of the tenth day after Pearson Tate's death. As they rode away, Seffleck screamed. 'I don't deserve this, Real Lee. I don't. If ever I get a chance, you'll pay. I swear you'll pay.'

'I've heard of men getting pardons,' Lilywhite said. 'That man should have died.'

'No one's ever escaped from Yuma,' Real said. 'It's a hell hole. Just what Seffleck deserves.'

A group of Payson's leading citizens approached. Fred Solomon spoke for them. 'Real Lee,' he said. 'We, the newly organized Payson council, think our city should have an officer of the law. We wish to hire you as the marshal of Payson. Will you take the job?'

Lilywhite said, 'Please, Real.'

Real Lee smiled. 'Does that mean I could kind of settle down here?'

It was Lilywhite's turn to smile. She didn't need to answer.

'Fred. I'd consider it an honor to be marshal of Payson. But I have one proviso.'

'You name it.'

'I'll need a good deputy,' Real said.

'Got anyone in mind?'

'If he'll take the job.'

'Who?'

'Lightning Brewster.'

Lightning's jaw dropped.

'How about it, Lightning? You willing to work on the

159

side of the law?'

'Sure,' Lightning said. 'I'd work with you anywhere. Do I get paid?'

Real laughed. 'Dollar a day,' he said.